Girl TALK

Best Friends

Have you seen all the
Best Friends
books?

A Challenge for
LAUREN

Heather Maisner

First published in 1998 by BBC Worldwide Ltd
Woodlands, 80 Wood Lane, London W12 0TT

Text by Heather Maisner copyright © BBC Worldwide Ltd 1998
The author asserts the moral right to be identified as the
author of the work.

Girl Talk copyright © BBC Worldwide Ltd 1995

ISBN 0 563 40553 8

Cover photography by Jamie Hughes

Thanks to Empire

Printed and bound by Mackays of Chatham plc

Let **Girl TALK** introduce you to the
greatest bunch of Best Friends ever...

First there's

Lauren
who's an
ace Swimmer

unlike

Cork
who admits
she'd rather help

Best
Friends

but she will need
a trendy costume
first!

Anya

that just leaves

Sunita

pull up weeds all day

Gemma

with

For Georgia and her friends.

With thanks to Mark and Iris Amor,
of Astra Swimming Club, Hammersmith.

Chapter 1

"**I**"m *so* bored!"

Lauren was lying stretched out on the carpet in front of the television, flicking from one TV station to another. She really wanted to be outside doing something energetic, but now the football season was over, she couldn't decide what to do.

Harry, her three-year-old brother, threw open the living room door. Pretending his arm was an elephant's trunk he charged towards her, trumpeting.

At the last moment, Lauren rolled sideways. Harry crashed into the sofa and began to wail.

Their mum stormed in from the kitchen.

"Sorry," yawned Lauren, not turning round.

"Oh Lauren," her mum exclaimed. "Why can't

you be kinder to your brother?"

"Because he is my brother," Lauren tossed her blonde pony tail. "And I'm bored."

As soon as she uttered the word, Lauren regretted it. Her mum never allowed *anyone* to be bored.

"Well, I'm sure there's plenty of homework you could be doing," Mrs Standish said. "And before that, you can empty the washing machine."

Lauren dragged herself to her feet and shuffled into the kitchen. She wondered why it was that the less you did, the less you felt able to do? She watched the clothes whirl round as the machine rattled to a standstill.

The shrill ring of the phone interrupted Lauren's day dreaming.

"I'll get it," she shouted to her mum. "I know you'd hate me to get bored waiting for the washing to finish!"

As she picked up the receiver, Harry grabbed the extension in the sitting room.

"Hello," said Lauren.

"Raaah," roared Harry.

"Hi," said another voice faintly down the line.

"Put it down, Harry, or I'll eat you," Lauren shouted and the extension telephone crashed back into its cradle.

"Wow, you're having fun!" Anya Michaels laughed. "I bet you're pleased there's no football tonight."

Lauren and Anya had known each other for years, although they now lived at opposite ends of town and went to different schools.

"Don't talk to me about it!" Lauren sighed. "I've got nothing to look forward to."

"Well…" Anya paused for effect. "I think I've got the answer."

"What?"

"There's a tap class starting at the Dance Centre soon. It sounds really cool. The teacher's famous, she's won loads of awards. She's danced in New York, Paris, all over the world! Astrid says…"

As soon as Anya mentioned her friend Astrid, Lauren yawned and started doodling on the telephone pad. Anya was forever telling stories about Astrid's famous dad and all the fabulous people he knew.

"Look," Lauren said when Anya paused for a moment, "I'm not into flapping about doing tap dancing. I can't be bothered with that kind of thing."

"But have you ever tried? I mean it is sort of physical and it must be better than staying at home with Harry."

"Yes. But…"

Across town in her pink and white bedroom, Anya held her white portable telephone to her ear. She wriggled her toes in her pink fluffy slippers and imagined how cute she would look in shiny black tap shoes. She was desperate to get her friends to join her at the classes.

"Lauren," she said. "Why don't you think about it while I ring the others? And maybe you could tell Gemma about it."

"OK. I'll go and see what she thinks."

As Lauren unloaded the washing machine and collected the laundry in from the garden, she started to come round to the idea of tap dancing – anything would be better than doing nothing. But when she strolled next door to tell her best friend Gemma about it, Gemma simply fell about laughing.

"Lauren, you must be joking," she spluttered. "I can't imagine you prancing about and tapping your toes. Can you?"

Lauren and Gemma had been friends since they were tiny. They'd been living next door to each other for ages now and were almost like sisters.

"But I have to do something to get out of the house. I'll go crazy if I'm stuck in there with Harry and the washing," said Lauren.

"But you won't be," Gemma told her. "The Sports Centre is about to open the new swimming pool. Hasn't your dad told you about it?"

"I thought it wouldn't be ready for months!" cried Lauren.

"Your dad told my dad. They've got a new coach and there's going to be a swimming gala and..."

"A *gala*? Are you sure?" Lauren's eyes opened wide. "Trust Dad to tell everyone except me!"

"Go and ask him yourself!" said Gemma, grinning.

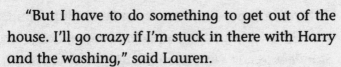

As soon as her father's key turned in the lock, Lauren rushed up to him.

"Dad, dad," she said. "Is the pool really opening this time? Is there going to be a swimming gala?"

"Calm down, calm down," her father laughed. "Didn't I tell you about the pool and the new coach we've got?"

"No, you didn't!" Lauren almost shouted. The pool had been closed for improvements for several months now and the opening had been delayed many times.

A Challenge for Lauren

"Well, the new man's name is Peter Clifton and, yes, he's organising a swimming gala," Mr Standish said. "We sent out a newsheet this week to all the district schools."

"Not to ours!" wailed Lauren.

"Well, anyway, the swimming club's starting up again tomorrow. I'm *sure* I told you about it…"

"You didn't," Lauren stated flatly. "You work there, but you never tell us anything."

"We're always the last to hear what's going on," her older brother Ben agreed. "Remember how you forgot to tell me when the Tennis Club started and I was nearly too late to join."

"And I almost missed out on trampoline classes when I was six," Lauren continued.

"Leave your dad alone," their mother Karen warned, darting meaningful looks at each of her three children. "Dad *is* forgetful, but you still get to hear about things the way most people do – through the grapevine. Anyway, he's got a lot on his plate."

Mr Standish smiled. "Yes and right now, I'd like sausage and egg on it! Is dinner ready yet Karen?"

Lauren was in a world of her own. "I can't wait to tell the others!"

Lauren called Anya back straight after supper.

"That's great! Hey, I've been talking to Astrid about the tap classes. They don't start for a few weeks so we can join the swimming club first then join the tap classes later."

"Well…" Lauren knew there was no chance she'd ever do tap now, but she didn't want to disappoint Anya. "Maybe," she said. "Anyway I'll see you at the pool tomorrow."

"Sure thing," Anya agreed. As soon as the receiver clicked, she threw the white phone onto her pretty pink bedspread and began to hunt through her drawers and cupboards for her new swimsuit.

Lauren tried Sunita next, hoping she wouldn't get her gran – old Mrs Banerjee always wanted to know why you were calling her precious Sunny.

Luckily, Sunita's mum answered. "Hold on, Lauren, I'll get her for you."

Lauren explained to Sunita about the swimming gala in an excited rush of words.

"Swimming lessons start tomorrow," she continued. "And, if we all get to the pool early, we can get in some practice before anyone else – then we can all be in the squad together and…"

"Wait a minute," Sunita broke in. "You don't really think my gran will agree to a swimming gala, do you? Anya's just phoned about tap classes and Gran almost had a fit. You know how she is, Lauren. And if *she* disapproves, so will Mum and Dad."

"You can at least ask her," Lauren persisted. "After all, swimming isn't anything like tap dancing. It's good for you! Just say you'll design a swimsuit that covers you head to toe so nothing shows. Go on, Sunita, we'd make a great team. *Please* ask."

Sunita didn't want to disappoint Lauren but she doubted whether her gran would think that training for a swimming gala was a worthwhile way to spend her time, not when there was always extra maths that could be done. And although Sunita quite liked swimming, she didn't want to lose precious time that could be spent on her real love – designing clothes. Even though she'd done really well in a fashion competition recently, her family still didn't really approve of her ambition to be a designer. They wanted Sunita to become an accountant.

"I'll come if I can," she said. "But don't hold out too much hope."

Lauren put down the phone and skipped out

through the back gate and into Gemma's garden.

"You again?" cried Gemma. "What are you doing, splashing or tapping?"

Gemma, who loved animals more than anything in the world, was feeding the rabbits with Carli, the fifth and latest member of their gang. Pets weren't allowed in the Fairlight estate where Carli lived, so her rabbit, Snowball, stayed here with Gemma's rabbit, Thumper.

"Gemma, Carli," Lauren ran up to them, bursting with her news. "The swimming pool is open and the club is starting up tomorrow. You've both got to come. You've just *got* to. We have to get in training for the gala."

"What's this 'we'?" asked Gemma. "You know I'm a lousy swimmer, Lauren. It takes me half an hour to get from one side of the pool to the other!"

"Well, you'll get faster if you practise," said Lauren.

"But there's no way I'll ever be good enough for a gala." Gemma poured dried food from a large sack into the rabbits' bowls while the pets hopped around the garden, nibbling at the grass. "Anyway, tomorrow's Saturday, and that's when I clean out the hutches..."

"Oh, come on Gems, you can clean them in the afternoon. Even Sunita is going to try and talk her

A Challenge for Lauren

gran round," Lauren rushed on. "And if we all go together, we can all be in the *club* together. And you said yourself that when I stopped playing football, we should all do something together. You *have* to come."

Gemma looked up at her friend. When Lauren wanted something really badly, she usually got her way. She had the kind of energy that made things happen, and Gemma loved her for it.

"All right, all right. I'll come," Gemma laughed. "But..." She looked around the garden. "Oh no! Thumper is trying to dig his way out again!" She hurtled off to stop the wayward rabbit.

Lauren turned to Carli, who had been quietly scraping carrots on the patio.

"You'll come, won't you?" she said. "You were ace at bowling that time, I bet you're ace at swimming, too. We'll have a real laugh."

"I'll try," Carli replied without looking up. "I'll ask my mum when I get home. I'll come if I can."

"Great! See ya! Bye, Gems!" With that, Lauren cartwheeled three times across the lawn, her long legs forming perfect circles. She skipped out through the gate and back into her house.

Had she looked back, Lauren might have seen Carli's pink and embarrassed face. Carli didn't want to let her friend down, but she hadn't told

Best Friends

Lauren the truth. She hadn't dared explain that she was actually terrified of water. Not only that, she'd grown out of her swimsuit and knew that her mother couldn't afford to buy her a new one. Mrs Pike was bringing up Carli and her younger sister Annie on her own with very little money, and Carli didn't want to upset her by even mentioning the subject. Her dad, who was going to get married again soon, had just bought her an expensive new pair of trainers, so she didn't want to ask him for anything else just yet.

Later, when her mum had called round to walk her home, she began to feel queasy. She looked miserably at the graffiti on the walls of the Fairlight estate as Mrs Pike pressed for the lift. As usual, it was broken.

Biting her lip, Carli climbed the two flights of stairs to the flat, worrying about what she was going to do. If all her friends were joining the swimming club, she'd hate to miss out, but the prospect of evening after evening at the pool seemed unbearable.

Chapter 2

"**Y**ou're up early for a Saturday," Mr Standish laughed, as Lauren rushed into the kitchen.

"That's 'cause you're taking me swimming," she reminded him, pulling her blonde hair into a high ponytail.

Lauren wolfed down some cereal, grabbed her swimming bag and ran next door to call for Gemma.

Mrs Gordon wearily opened the door, still in her dressing gown. "Gemma's just getting dressed," she mumbled. "Come in and wait."

"Dad says the new pool looks brilliant, Mrs Gordon," gabbled Lauren, following her into the kitchen. "And we want to be first to see it, don't we Gems?"

"We don't. *You* do," Gemma yawned as she

came through the kitchen door, rubbing her eyes. She poured cereal into a bowl, spilling half of it over the table.

"Come on slug, eat up and let's go," Lauren said.

"The pool's not going anywhere, Lauren!" answered Gemma, grinning at her friend through a mouthful of rice crispies.

"Neither are we, that's the problem," moaned Lauren. "Come *on*!"

"All right, all right! I have to get my swimsuit." Gemma thumped upstairs, still crunching cereal between her teeth.

Northborough Sports Centre had been completely changed. There was a new beginners' pool and a fun area with fountains and a wave machine. A long, curved chute led into a deep pool next to it, and spectator benches had been built around the extended main pool. The hall had been painted bright blue, with yellow and purple swirls across the ceiling.

"It's fantastic!" Lauren exclaimed.

"Well cool," Gemma agreed. "Get those colours! Sunita will be reaching for her sketchpad the moment she walks in!"

19

A Challenge for Lauren

The pool was silent, the water calm and inviting.

"And it's all for us. Come on," said Lauren, pulling on her swimming cap. She dived in the deep end and swam underwater for ages before surfacing. Gemma jumped in after her with a splash.

But they didn't have the pool to themselves for long. The reopening had attracted crowds of people. In a very short time the water rippled and churned with the movement of bodies and the hall echoed with the sound of their voices. Lauren wondered how many were going to be trying out for the gala.

A pretty dark-haired girl wearing a bikini moved towards the water. She stood at the poolside, scrunching up her nose and twiddling her plaits, searching the swimmers' faces.

"Anya! Anya!" Gemma called, jumping up and down in the shallow end.

Lauren waved her arms and shouted, "We're over here."

Anya sauntered towards them, tidying the straps on her bikini top and making sure the buckle on her shorts was hanging at the right angle.

"This place is cool, isn't it?" she said. "Astrid

won't believe it when I tell her."

"Anya, what are you wearing?" Lauren asked, hoisting herself out of the pool.

"Isn't it great!" Anya's eyes sparkled. "As soon as I saw it, I knew I had to have it." She spun round to give her friends a better view of her denim blue bikini.

"This isn't a beach party, you know," said Lauren, a little crossly. "You want to get picked for the gala, don't you?"

"Of course I do," Anya retorted. "What's that got to do with it?"

"No one ever races in a bikini!" Lauren frowned. "Belts and buckles slow you down. You're just not being serious."

"Look, if you don't want me to be here, I'll go home." Anya started to walk away.

Gemma quickly stepped in front of Anya. "All Lauren means is that you'll swim much faster if you wear something simple. Come on, Anya, you know you like going fast."

"You mean I need a streamline swimsuit?" Anya's eyes cleared and brightened.

"Yes," said Lauren, nodding. "That's what I was trying to say."

"Maybe I can get my dad to buy me a new Speedo one." Anya was the only child by her dad's

21

second marriage and he adored her. Sometimes her friends teased her about being spoilt, but today, Lauren was pleased.

"Brill!" she said. "Now get in and I'll race you to the end of the pool!"

"This had better work," grumbled Sunita as she staggered around the house with the vacuum cleaner, keeping an eye on the clock. She'd decided her gran might let her go to see the new pool if she showed how good she was by helping with the housework. She'd been hoovering, dusting and polishing for almost two hours.

"It's now or never," Sunita muttered to herself. She put the vacuum cleaner away and strolled in to the kitchen.

"I've done everything *Dadima*," she said. "I was just thinking that I might…"

"Good, good," said Mrs Banerjee Senior. "Mrs Rahmani and her family are coming for lunch. I'm making so many dishes, I could do with some help. Be a good girl and peel these mangoes for me…"

Sunita sighed, slouching over the kitchen counter in despair. There was absolutely no way she would make it down to the pool now.

"Where are they?" grumbled Lauren. "There's no sign of Sunita *or* Carli!"

"I guess Sunita couldn't get past her gran," Anya said.

"And maybe Carli couldn't get a lift," Gemma mused. "Her mum doesn't have a car."

Just then, the new coach appeared and blew his whistle to call everyone to the shallow end of the pool. He smoothed back his shiny dark hair while he waited, looking fit and handsome in a green tracksuit.

"Hi," he said. "Welcome to the new pool. My name is Peter Clifton…"

"He looks really nice," Anya said, elbowing Gemma in the ribs. "Look at the muscles on his arms!"

"I like his eyes," said Gemma, trying not to giggle.

"…And as I'm sure you all know, we'll be holding a gala here at the end of July," Peter continued. "It'll be the biggest event in the county."

Behind him, a large girl with thick, black hair strode towards the pool, gossiping loudly to two other girls. It was Alex Marshall, the biggest bully at Duston Middle School, with her cronies Charlotte Derring and Marga De Santos. Alex

A Challenge for Lauren

looked around at the new décor and sneered. "Don't think much of them colours, do you Marga?"

"What's *she* doing here?" whispered Lauren.

"Causing trouble, I expect," answered Gemma, raising her eyes to Anya. They'd had more than one run-in with Alex in the past.

Alex jumped into the pool with a loud splash, her two friends following her, then she pushed her way to the front of the swimmers. Peter waited until the pool quietened down again, then he continued.

"Today I want you all to show me what you can do. Over the next few weeks I'll be organising training sessions. We don't have much time, but if we work hard and pull together I feel sure that we can make Northborough Swimming Club the best in the district."

He smiled at them, outlining his plans, and suddenly everyone was smiling back. Even Alex nodded her head and grinned at her friends. And Gemma, who knew that she wasn't a good swimmer, felt that if she tried really hard, she might make it into a team. Anything seemed possible with Peter as the coach.

"Now I want you to line up in front of the lanes and swim one length each," Peter said. "Use any stroke you like. But I expect everyone who wants to be in the squad to be able to do the four main strokes – breaststroke, front crawl, back crawl and butterfly."

The children climbed out of the water and lined up as Peter had instructed them. Lauren, who couldn't wait to show off her skills, was the first swimmer in lane one. Anya, standing behind her, tightened the straps on her bikini as she waited her turn. Gemma stood behind Anya biting her lip. She didn't know how to do butterfly stroke, but if she was fast enough at the others, maybe Lauren – or Peter – could help her.

At the front of lane two, level with Lauren, Alex Marshall shoved her thick hair into a tight red swimming cap and pulled down her goggles. When Peter shouted, "On your marks," she flashed Lauren a determined look. At "Go!" the girls dived in together. They swam level with each other and reached the other end almost at the same time. Lauren felt sure that her fingers touched the end wall first, but Alex quickly hoisted herself out on to the poolside and put up her hand.

"I was first!" she bellowed at Peter. Then she fixed Lauren with a fierce stare. "You'll need to speed up, Lauren Standish, if you're going to keep up with me," she sneered.

At the end of the session, Peter called the swimmers together once again. "That was great!" he said. "Well done, *all* of you. But we'll need to put in lots of training before we're ready to compete against other clubs. This week I want you to come to the pool as often as you can. Next week I'll choose the squad – about forty people to compete in the gala. And of course I'll be choosing the captains."

Lauren felt her head buzzing. 'Please, let me be one,' she prayed silently.

After training the three friends stayed on to enjoy the fun session. They messed around on a huge monster inflatable, pushing each other off; were tossed around by the wave machine, and then spent ages speeding down the enormous chute. Finally, they dragged themselves away to get dressed and dry their hair.

"This place is fantastic," Lauren said, beaming.

"It's brilliant," agreed Anya. "I really want to be in the squad, don't you? I mean, this beats tap dancing any day."

"Even with the most famous dance teacher in the world?" teased Lauren, ducking to avoid the towel Anya swiped at her.

"I wish I swam more like a dolphin and less like a demented cat," Gemma moaned, pulling a red

A Challenge for Lauren

plastic comb through her dark bob.

"What about Alex?" moaned Lauren. "She swims like a dolphin and she's built like a whale!"

The girls burst out laughing, glancing over their shoulders to check Alex wasn't too close. "Oh well," said Gemma. "Whatever happens – I'm really glad I came."

When they left the Sports Centre, two teenage boys were waiting outside. One had a shaved head and a small goatee beard, the other had thick black curtains of hair. They were Alex Marshall's big brothers, Aaron and Zack.

"How did it go?" Aaron called out to his sister as she came through the door. "Are you the best? Did you make the squad?"

"Of course I'm the best," Alex answered. "But they don't choose the squad until next week."

"I'll give you some coaching," said Zack. "This gala's going to be in the local papers and on TV. You don't want to settle for being in the squad, Alex. You want to be captain."

Lauren and her friends hurried past trying not to attract too much attention to themselves. If Alex was the biggest bully at Duston Middle School, her brothers were far worse. They had a growing reputation as real trouble-makers all over town. No one wanted to get too close to them.

A Challenge for Lauren

When they were out of earshot, Anya immediately turned to her friends, "Did you hear that? TV and newspapers! We've *got* to be in the squad, all of us. The others have *got* to come."

"Good luck explaining that to Sunita's gran," said Gemma. Then she frowned. "I wonder what happened to Carli?"

Back home, Gemma decided to try and find out exactly why Carli had let them down. Her mum dropped her at the Fairlight estate and waited in the car below until Gemma waved goodbye from the second floor balcony. Gemma didn't like going alone to the flats. They were cold and unfriendly, making her feel edgy.

Mrs Pike opened the door a little and peered through the crack to see who was there, before taking off the chain.

"Oh, hello, Gemma," she smiled. "Carli will be pleased to see you. She's been stuck indoors with Annie all day."

"Is that why she didn't come swimming?" Gemma asked.

"Swimming? She didn't mention that," Mrs Pike frowned. "She volunteered to play with Annie so that I could have a rest."

She led the way to Carli's room, and Gemma knocked on the door. "Carli, can I come in?"

Carli swung the door open at once, blinking behind her pink plastic glasses. "Oh, hi, Gemma."

Her little sister Annie leapt off the bed. "All right Gemma! Carli's been painting my face. How do I look?"

"Like a leopard," said Gemma. "It's wicked!"

Gemma sat beside Carli on her bed in the little room, while Annie chattered away about what they'd been doing. Whenever Gemma tried to talk to Carli, Annie's voice got louder and louder. In the end, she was persuaded to fetch them all something to drink.

"Sisters! Pains, aren't they? Lucy still drives me nuts!" Gemma laughed once the door was closed. "Is that why you didn't come swimming? Because of Annie?"

"I just wanted to look after her this morning, that's all," Carli shrugged, not looking at Gemma.

Something was wrong. Carli was being as defensive as when she first joined Duston Middle School and was being picked on by Alex.

"You should have seen the pool," Gemma chatted on, hoping that Carli's mood would lift. "You won't believe how much it's changed. And the new coach Peter is fantastic. You really ought to come. There's not a problem, is there...?"

"Gemma, everything's fine, OK? I just couldn't come."

"But you didn't even ask your mum, did you?"

Carli looked startled. Just then Annie opened the door, laden with tumblers of lemonade. "Carli's too scared to go swimming," she announced.

Carli turned on her sister. "Shut it, you!"

"She can hardly swim." Annie was thrilled to get Gemma's attention again. "And her swimsuit's too small. *Look*!" Annie reached into a drawer and pulled out a faded pink costume.

Carli snatched the swimsuit out of her hands and shoved it under the bed. "If you don't shut up I won't let you near my face paints *ever* again!"

Gemma quickly changed the subject. "Well... You wouldn't *believe* how much lettuce the rabbits got through this morning! You'd think I never fed them!"

"How much?" Carli asked, her eyes widening.

Gradually, as the girls chatted away and Annie went off to watch a cartoon, Carli started to get more cheerful. At the end of the afternoon, Gemma decided to steer the conversation back to swimming.

"I've got an idea," she said. "Annie could come over and play with Lucy next Saturday. Lucy would love it and I'm sure Mum wouldn't mind. Then you can come to the pool and we can all be together."

"I'm not a charity case, you know," Carli snapped.

"I know you're not. You're just one of my best friends," said Gemma, simply. She and Carli linked fingers and whispered their gang's special chant.

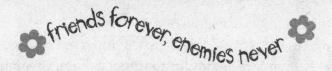

friends forever, enemies never

Gemma grinned at Carli. "It'll be great, honestly. They've got a beginners' pool, where I'm going to learn butterfly stroke. If we can find you a swimsuit, maybe we could learn together? I'm sure Lauren will help us, she was great when I started swimming."

As Gemma walked home later, she felt much happier. It didn't seem fair that Carli had spent the day indoors – she knew they could help her overcome her fear of water. If she had her way, the whole gang would be in the swimming club together after all...

Chapter 3

On Wednesday, after school, Sunita, Gemma, Carli and Anya met in front of the large department store in town. Lauren was busy swimming.

"All right girls," said Mrs Michaels, Anya's mum. "I'll pick you up in half an hour, OK?"

"OK, Mum!" said Anya, sweetly, before turning round and rolling her eyes to her friends. "You'd think we were six-year-olds or something," she muttered.

"Maybe it's 'cause you act like one too often!" teased Sunita.

"I'll ignore that pathetic remark," said Anya, coolly.

Together, they wandered through the jewellery section on the ground floor. "I'm thinking of getting my ears pierced," said Anya.

"They *are* pierced," Gemma reminded her.

"Yeah, but I want more holes down the side," Anya pulled back her long dark hair to reveal one perfectly-shaped ear.

"Why stop at ears?" Carli teased. "What about your nose and lips?"

"Or even your belly button?" Sunita added.

Anya made to elbow Sunita, then stopped as she saw a salesgirl with sample perfumes.

"Brilliant, look. Perfume," she said, holding out her arm for a spray from the tester bottle. "I *love* perfume!"

"Me too," said Sunita, extending her arm. "Here you go, Carli, have a spray yourself!"

Carli wrinkled up her nose. "No, let me try that one. Hey, careful, Anya, you've clouded up my glasses!"

Gemma giggled and coughed at the same time, grabbing the others. "We'd better move on, before we stink out the whole store!"

They took the escalator to the fashion department where Sunita wanted to stop and browse, but Anya urged them on.

"We'll look later," she said. "We've got to get to the swimwear before the store closes!"

She dragged them off towards the swimsuits and

began to pick out an armful that she liked.

Gemma shook her head, frowning. "They're all too fancy. Maybe we should try the sports shop down the road."

They dashed out of the store – Sunita grabbing one quick look at the latest dresses on the way – and ran to Northborough Sports.

"Just in time," panted Carli, flicking through the rail of costumes. "There's not a lot of choice though, is there? I think I'd rather wear my old pink number!"

Gemma beamed at her. She was pleased Carli could joke about her problems with them.

"We've got a big delivery coming on Friday," said the man at the cash desk. "All the latest swimming gear. Why don't you come back then?"

"But what if the new stuff's as bad as that lot?" Anya moaned as they walked away.

"You'll just have to ask Sunita to design a costume for you!" said Carli.

"Now *that's* a good idea," Sunita grinned. "I'll add a swimwear section to my new collection!"

The whole of the Standish family knew it was

A Challenge for Lauren

Saturday because Lauren was tearing around the house like a whirlwind.

"Look, today is *really* important," she said, bumping into her brother Ben for the third time. "Peter's going to choose the squad!"

"Oh, the great Peter!" Ben teased as Lauren disappeared next door to call for Gemma.

Gemma's dad was cooking his usual morning fry-up and teasing his daughter, who had recently turned vegetarian. "If you want to be a swimmer," he told her, "you need to eat lots of protein and that means meat."

"You can get protein from other things besides meat, Dad," Gemma replied wearily. "There are *masses* of good things, like..."

"We haven't got time to talk about them now," Lauren butted in. "Hurry up, Gems. We have to go!"

They were on their way out of the door, when Carli turned up with her sister Annie.

"I'm coming along to watch," Carli grinned. "I don't want to be the only person in town who hasn't seen the new pool or met Mr Magnificent the coach."

"That's great!" said Lauren, hugging her. "I really do want us all to be together!"

35

A Challenge for Lauren

When they got inside the Sports Centre Lauren and Gemma hurried to get ready while Carli climbed up on to the spectator benches. Eventually Anya appeared, wearing a pale blue streamline swimsuit with a high neck.

"You look amazing," Lauren shouted.

"I feel ready to swim like a fish," Anya cried. "Dad took me to the sports shop yesterday. The new gear is wicked!"

"You look brill!" Carli said, climbing down from the benches to chat with the girls at the poolside.

"So will you, in a minute," Anya said. "I've brought you this."

She lifted the towel over her arm to reveal a deep blue swimsuit with stars on it.

"It's too small for me. Dad bought it for me last year but I hardly wore it."

"But, but..." Carli blushed and looked away. She didn't want to accept hand-me-downs from her friends. Nor did she really want to swim.

"You've got to try it on," Gemma insisted. "Anya brought it along specially. Come on, we all want to see what it looks like on you."

The girls ushered Carli into the changing rooms

before she could say another word in protest, and waited in suspense.

Earlier in the week, when Gemma had suggested that Anya might like to give her old costume to Carli, Anya hadn't been sure whether she wanted to part with it. Now, as Anya saw Carli wearing it, she smiled with pleasure. "Doesn't Carli look great?" she said, beaming. "It's a perfect fit!"

"It's the nicest swimsuit I've ever worn," Carli said, but then she bit her lip and a small crease worked its way into her pale brow. "But you have to take it back, because... Well, because I really *don't* want to swim today." She looked nervously at the pool with its crowd of splashing swimmers.

"It's like I said before, Carli," said Gemma, quickly taking her friend's elbow. "You can start off in the beginners' pool."

"Yeah, take your time – it's really shallow in there," added Lauren.

"I used to be terrified of the water," said Gemma. "But Lauren forced me to keep going. It's a good laugh once you're used to it."

Lauren led the way and the three girls jumped into the beginners' pool with Carli. Gemma went to find the floats and threw them into the water.

"I want the rubber duck," Anya shouted.

"And I want the turtle!" Lauren jumped up and

caught it.

"Here, Carli, you take this." Gemma handed Carli a flat white float and took one for herself.

They glided around, kicking their legs and splashing each other. Lauren helped Gemma with her butterfly stroke, until Peter blew the whistle and the swimmers went back to the main pool, leaving Carli to practise with the float.

Peter held up his hand for silence.

"Today, I want you to divide yourselves into age groups," he said. "And I'm going to time you as you swim each of the four main strokes. At the end of the session, I'll pick the squad, the people who will train for the gala. Later, when we know who's best at what, I'll divide the squad into teams – and I'll also be picking team captains, one for the boys and one for the girls." Peter brushed his fingers through his hair. "By the way – I think we need a new name. Northborough Swimming Club isn't very exciting. We need a logo for posters and T-shirts. If anyone's got any bright ideas, I want to hear them!"

Shouting and jostling, the swimmers divided themselves into age groups. They came from lots of different schools in the area, so although nearly everyone knew at least one other person, they didn't all know each other.

"Try and keep the noise down!" Peter called. "We haven't got all day!"

Lauren, Gemma and Anya managed to stay close together. Nearby they also noticed Alex, Charlotte and Marga. Despite the number of children milling around waiting to swim, it seemed that Alex was constantly at Lauren's elbow. At one point, she nudged Lauren out of the way and muscled in ahead of her so that she could swim first.

"Ignore her," Gemma advised Lauren.

"Why should I?" Lauren exploded. "Why's she doing it?"

"Because she knows you're such a good swimmer," Anya said. "She's trying to put you off. Stay out of her way."

Between turns, Lauren wandered over to the beginners' pool to chat to Carli. She even got in the pool with her, teaching Carli breathing exercises by holding the rail and ducking her head into the water.

Carli ducked down, but came up spluttering. "I can't... I can't do it!" she said.

"Of course you can," Lauren insisted. "Don't panic. Nothing can happen. I'm standing right beside you."

After a few tries, Carli stopped spluttering. "It's

A Challenge for Lauren

not so bad, when you get the hang of it," she said, smiling. "Thanks, Lauren."

"Don't worry – actually it's taking my mind off the squad selection," she smiled nervously. "I suppose I'd better go back now though." Lauren raised herself out of the water and headed off to join the others.

"Good luck Lauren!" Carli shouted after her friend.

Back at the main pool, tension was mounting as the swimmers waited for Peter to make his decision. At last, he called them all together.

"With so many good swimmers here, it's been difficult to decide," he began, his eyes scanning down the clipboard he held. "And I hope that those who aren't chosen today won't be too disappointed. If you haven't made the squad now, there's always next time. Remember, this is only the beginning. We have many weeks of training ahead of us. A good team depends on all its members. So if anyone feels they'll have trouble making it to all the practice sessions, let me know straightaway." He looked seriously at the crowd of eager swimmers. Then he began to read out the names in alphabetical order.

Charlotte Derring, Alex's friend, was the first name the gang recognised. She jumped up and punched the air. Tania James, who also went to Duston Middle School was the next. Her friend Katie Kelly had also been chosen.

Gemma soon realised that she hadn't been picked. For a moment, she felt disappointed. Her cheeks flushed with embarrassment as her friends shot her sympathetic glances.

"Never mind, guys," she shrugged. "It's OK." Although it stung to be left out, Gemma realised that she had known all along that she didn't have much of a chance.

When Alex Marshall's name came up, she let out a whoop of joy and looked round triumphantly. Anya heard her own name and clapped her hands.

"I can't wait to tell Astrid," she whispered. Then she added quickly, "I'll tell her I'm joining the club until tap classes begin."

"Tap's nothing! This is everything!" muttered Lauren, waiting tensely for Peter to reach the letter S. Not for the first time, she wished that her surname began with an A. When her name was finally read out, her face broke into smiles. Gemma and Anya both hugged her, then they all ran across to share the news with Carli.

Peter clapped his hands for silence again, and the girls wandered back to join the crowd.

"Now, about the captains I've chosen," he said. "A captain needs to be someone who not only performs well but also has the ability to recognise the skills of others and to encourage them. Someone who is able to get on with everyone. A captain has to hold the team together and make it work. For the girls' team, I have chosen..."

The crowd strained forward eagerly. Peter waited a second, then grinned and pronounced the name:

"Lauren Standish."

Lauren gasped and covered her mouth. "*Yes!*" cried Gemma, leaping into the air. But Alex Marshall scowled, turning her back on Lauren, and pushed her way through the crowd.

As the girls chatted excitedly in the changing rooms, Alex strode up to Lauren and poked her finger into her face.

"You think you're really someone, don't you?" she spat. "Well, you're not. You don't have what it takes to win a real race."

"What are you on about, Alex?" Lauren began, but Charlotte barged in.

"That Peter's a lousy coach," she said. "He

doesn't know what he's doing. He only made you captain because your dad works here."

"Yeah," Marga added from behind them. "He wants to keep on the good side of your dad, don't he? That's the only reason he picked you."

"You're Pete's pet," Alex sneered.

Lauren took a deep breath and looked like she was going to go for Alex, but Gemma quickly stepped in front of her and grabbed her arm.

"Don't listen to Alex," she said, glaring defiantly. "She's just jealous."

"And I'm starving," said Anya, in a weak attempt to change the subject.

"Let's get some chips in the canteen before they sell out," Carli agreed, avoiding Alex's eyes.

Her friends hurried her away, but the joy had suddenly drained out of Lauren's day. Was that *really* the reason why she'd been made captain? Because of her dad?

Chapter 4

"It was Sunday morning and Gemma lay in bed thinking about yesterday's swimming. She hadn't really expected to be picked for the squad, but still couldn't help feeling a bit left out. To take her mind off it, she tried to think up a name for the club instead. She got a pen and a scrap of paper and started scribbling a list of ideas. She was just reading them out loud to herself when there was a tap on the door and her mum walked in.

"Mum, Mum, listen," said Gemma, eagerly, sitting up. "I've thought up loads of names for the swimming club." She started reading them out. "I like the Dolphins, best. What do you think?"

"That sounds good," Mrs Gordon smiled. "Why don't you try it out on Lauren, see if she wants her team to be known as dolphins!"

"I'll phone her now." Gemma pulled back the bedcovers and headed for the door.

"While you're at it, Gems," her mother called after her, "how about asking her to come over and help you this morning."

"Help me do what?"

"Clear up Mrs Crick's garden."

"Eh?" Gemma turned round in surprise.

"Her son-in-law can't come over and she's desperate," Mrs Gordon explained. "So I said you'd pop across with some friends. Sorry Gems, but you often ask me what you can do on a Sunday. I thought that you probably wouldn't mind."

Gemma scrunched up her nose. "Nice one, Mum. Thanks a *lot*. Mrs Crick's a right old boot. She's always watching and waiting for you to do something wrong."

"I know, love," her mum said. "But Mr Crick only died last year, and it's hard for her now. Anyway, her dog, Nelson, will be around. You can play with him."

Gemma sighed. "That's something I suppose. Don't worry, Mum, I'll do it. I just hope the others will help me!"

Lauren and her family were just going out.

"Look, Gems, even if I wasn't busy this morning, why should I slave away for an old ratbag like Mrs Crick? I'll see you later so we can get that stupid homework done."

"But Lauren, I've thought of a great name for the…"

"Later!" called Lauren, plonking down the receiver.

"Yeah," muttered Gemma. "Later." The summer term's school project was called 'Changes', and the girls all had to make family trees to show how their families had grown over the generations. Anya was coming round too, as she had to get started on *her* school project.

Gemma still had to do Mrs Crick's garden before then, but luckily Carli and Sunita were more than willing to help. Carli had gone round to the Banerjees to help Sunita with her maths before going on to Lauren's, but they were both getting bored. Luckily, helping an old lady who lived alone was exactly the sort of activity Mrs Banerjee Senior approved of.

"I think you've found the one thing in the world

that could get me off my extra maths training!" said Sunita. "With the three of us working together we can have a bit of fun!"

"Thanks Sunita," said Gemma, smiling. "What would I do without you?"

Anya, however, had other things on her mind. She'd planned to meet up with Astrid and tell her all about the swimming club, and had no desire to change her plans in order to do gardening. "That sounds like a really sad way to spend the morning," she said.

"Some friend you are," Gemma retorted.

"Look Gems, my gardening skills aren't up to much and I can't stand that little rat Nelson."

"OK, OK. Enough," she laughed. "You're as bad as Lauren! I don't know, you top swimmers..."

"Give me long division any day!" wailed Sunita.

She, Gemma and Carli were pulling weeds and picking up litter from Mrs Crick's garden. It was hard, hot work, and Mrs Crick was making it even more difficult.

"Don't touch the flowers, girls," she said, fussily. "And mind those small plants. Don't step on any seedlings, will you. Oh, and do be careful about

that bush, Gemma."

She went in and out of the house, but continued to peep out at them through the curtains. The girls tried not to laugh, but each time Mrs Crick turned her back, they burst into giggles. It was difficult to do the job properly with someone constantly fussing over them.

"What do you think we should charge for this?" whispered Sunita.

"Shhh!" hissed Gemma, grinning.

After a while they gathered up the weeds and carried them through the side gate into the back garden. Nelson yapped after the girls.

"Shut the gate!" cried Mrs Crick. "Don't let Nelson out or he might run away!"

"Some loss that would be!" Carli joked.

"How would we manage without him?" sighed Sunita.

The friends worked hard, but the day got hotter. Soon they were really beginning to sweat.

"Is this a flower or a weed?" asked Carli, pointing with a trowel to a spindly plant.

"It had better be a weed," said Gemma. "I've dug up loads of them!"

They were in stitches, when Mrs Crick called through the window. "I'll bring you some cordial. Keep an eye on Nelson." The girls flopped down on the grass to rest.

"Hey, did I tell you I'd thought up a name for the swimming club?" Gemma asked.

"I have, too," said Carli.

"OK. Tell me the names," said Sunita. "And I'll say which I like best."

"The Dolphins!" Carli and Gemma shouted almost at the same time. Then they sat up and clapped their hands together.

"Wow, we both thought of the same name. How weird!" laughed Gemma. "Peter has *got* to like it."

Mrs Crick came hurrying out for the hundredth time. "Why are you shouting? What's happened?" she asked. Her eyes darted round the garden. "Where's Nelson?"

"He's in the bushes by the fence," Gemma said. "Isn't he?"

But when they looked, he wasn't there. They walked round the garden calling his name, and Mrs Crick fussed around searching the house, but the little dog didn't seem to be anywhere.

"He must have found a hole in the fence," said Sunita.

"You stupid, naughty girls! I told you to watch him," Mrs Crick shouted.

"We're really sorry," Gemma began. "We…"

But Mrs Crick was too worried to listen. "Get

out. Go on, *now*! You have to find my little Nelson. You have to bring my baby back!"

Gemma, Sunita and Carli ran desperately up and down the street looking for Nelson. They called out his name and knocked on people's doors, but nobody had seen him.

"This isn't getting us anywhere," said Gemma. "I think we should go and tell my mum."

Panting, sweaty and exhausted, they headed back, checking every bush and parked car, until they reached Gemma's house.

"We don't know where he went," Gemma explained.

"He just suddenly disappeared," Sunita added.

"And he isn't around anywhere," Carli said, shaking her head.

"Right. First of all, I'll get you a cold drink and you can all calm down," decided Mrs Gordon. "Nelson must be about somewhere. I'll phone some neighbours and tell the local shops to keep their eyes open."

Mrs Gordon poured some glasses of juice, then flicked through her address book and made several phone calls. The three girls tried to work out a plan of action. Every time a dog barked in the street or they heard the screech of a car braking sharply, one of them leapt up and ran to the window.

A Challenge for Lauren

Across the street, Mrs Crick's curtains twitched, as she also peered out anxiously.

"Don't worry," Mrs Gordon told them. "Nelson's most probably having a little adventure and will come back home when he's hungry. Right now we should keep exploring around here."

By the afternoon, there was still no sign of him. Mrs Gordon suggested they pass the time getting on with their project as planned, so the three friends sadly trooped next door to Lauren's house.

As they unpacked their folders in the Standishes' dining room, no one felt in the mood for homework. Lauren, who found drawing difficult at the best of times, kept on making a mess of her family tree. She drew it out in pencil and then tried to ink in the lines, but the ink went blotchy and she kept having to start again.

"What do you think about the 'Northborough Dolphins' as a name for the swimming club, Lauren?" asked Gemma.

"Mmm. Cool," said Lauren distractedly, but she wasn't really listening. She couldn't stop thinking about what Alex Marshall had said the day before, and once again her family tree was ruined. "Oh, this is hopeless," she said, scrunching up the paper. "I can't draw."

"I'll help you," Carli volunteered. "You just need

A Challenge for Lauren

to concentrate harder."

"I can't concentrate on anything after what happened at swimming," Lauren began. "I mean I was feeling really good about being made captain, but then..."

"Wait a minute," Gemma interrupted and ran to the window. "I thought I heard a dog bark. It could be Nelson."

"Oh, who cares about stupid Nelson!" Lauren spat out the words. "He's bound to turn up sooner or later. Anyway the street is much quieter without his yapping."

"You can say that again," Anya agreed. "I never could stand the little rat. He doesn't even look like a dog."

"How can you be so heartless?" protested Gemma.

"Look, it's our fault he ran away, Lauren," said Sunita.

"It's not *my* fault," Lauren snapped.

"Or mine," chipped in Anya, quickly.

"But us three are all really worried," Carli said. In a quiet voice, she went on. "Why don't we all work out what to say on a 'Missing Dog' notice. Something like, 'Chihuahua called Nelson. Last seen Sunday morning. Noisy but friendly...'"

"That's not true," Anya interrupted, shaking her

head. "He isn't friendly. He's ferocious."

"He's a pain," Lauren agreed, leaping to her feet. "And all this is a pain, too."

"You're being the pain, Lauren," said Gemma, regretting the words as soon as she said them.

Lauren stared at her in disbelief. "I have to listen to this stuff about a stupid dog, but nobody cares about what's worrying *me*!" She flung her felt-tip pen down on to her paper and stormed out of the room.

Gemma tried to follow her, but she was stopped by Sunita. "Don't, Gems," she said. "I don't think anything you say will help right now."

"Maybe I can persuade her to come back," Carli offered. She followed Lauren upstairs where she found her lying on her bed.

"Come on, Lauren," Carli said. "Gemma didn't mean it. You know what she's like about animals."

"But I'm so angry," Lauren exclaimed. "Nobody even wants to hear what's bothering me."

"We do, Lauren. Honest. Come down and I'm sure everyone will listen."

The girls immediately stopped what they were doing when Lauren reappeared at the door.

"Sorry, everyone," she said, taking a deep breath.

"No, *I'm* sorry," said Gemma. "I didn't mean it."

"I probably am a pain, right now," moped Lauren. "It's just... well... I can't believe how spiteful Alex was yesterday. I mean, I was so happy when Peter made me captain of the squad, but she ruined it for me." She slumped down on the sofa. "Do you think she could be right? Do you think Peter chose me as captain because of my dad?"

"That's *so* stupid," Anya said at once. "Don't take any notice of a loser like Alex."

"Like Gemma said yesterday, she's only jealous," added Sunita.

"Peter said a captain should encourage others," Carli added. "And that's what you do. You really helped me at the pool yesterday."

Gemma went over and gave Lauren a hug. "He wouldn't have chosen you if you weren't any good," she said. "He wants the club to win. He's mad for it, you know that."

"Yeah, I suppose he is," agreed Lauren. Then she grinned. "And so am I! I feel a hundred times better now. In fact, I feel so good that I think I could even go out and look for that horrible dog."

"Fantastic!" Gemma laughed. "Come on, then, let's go. Together we can do *anything*!"

They stood up and formed a circle, linked their little fingers together and chanted their special saying.

A Challenge for Lauren

❀ friends forever, enemies never ❀

Although the girls spent the rest of the afternoon searching the park and the streets, they couldn't find Nelson anywhere.

"My feet are aching," whinged Anya. "I have to stop." She was wearing new sandals that cut into her ankles.

"We'll leave you here, then," said Sunita. "Bye!"

"You *know* that's not what I meant," sulked Anya.

"It's getting dark anyway," sighed Carli.

"Come on, let's head back," said Lauren. Anya limped after the others as they slowly walked away.

"I won't be able to sleep tonight," Gemma worried, when they were back at Lauren's. "I keep thinking Nelson's been run over."

"Of course, he hasn't," Lauren told her. "You couldn't hit that squirmy little rat if you tried!"

"Lauren!" chided Sunita, giggling.

"Well, he's probably having the time of his life," Lauren added, defensively.

"And we can go searching again tomorrow after school," said Carli.

"If I can still walk, that is," Anya groaned.

Chapter 5

"**M**um, I need a new swimming bag," said Lauren between mouthfuls of cereal. "A really smart one."

Mrs Standish smiled at her daughter. She hadn't seen her in such a happy mood since the end of the football season.

"And Mum..."

"Yes?" she asked.

Lauren frowned as if she'd forgotten what she was going to say. Then her face lit up again and she sang out: "I'm captain!"

"Who cares?" her older brother Ben complained, as he grabbed some bread and dropped it into the toaster. "Give it a rest. You're giving me a headache." But Lauren simply continued to grin.

She kept on smiling even though Gemma and

Sunita were really gloomy on the way to school. Lauren knew they felt upset and guilty about Nelson, who was still missing, but she was so excited about being captain, she could barely think of anything else.

After assembly, Ms Drury swung into the classroom wearing Egyptian sandals and blue cotton trousers that billowed around her legs. Her bright red hair formed a wild sculpture of curls and metal clips.

She beamed at her class. "Rumour has it that my class has some exciting sports news!"

"That's right, Miss!" cried Katie. "Loads of us are in the swimming squad!"

"And Lauren's captain!" added Gemma.

"Well done, Lauren," said Ms Drury. "You've always been excellent at sports. Congratulations!"

"What about Alex and Charlotte?" Marga shouted out from the back of the class. "They're both in the squad too."

"I want to congratulate *everyone* in the squad," Ms Drury went on, ignoring Marga's outburst. "You have all done extremely well and I hope you will continue to do so. Now, everyone sit down and put your bags on the floor. It's time to exercise your *brains*, right now…"

At lunch, Lauren, Gemma, Sunita and Carli

huddled together in the playground discussing Nelson and their after-school plans. Other girls drifted over to join them.

"If anyone hears Nelson yapping or sees anything, you've got to tell me," Gemma begged them. She was white-faced and tired – she had hardly slept a wink last night.

"My aunt said there was a dead dog in the High Street," said Christie Brown, pushing forward. Everyone turned to look at her. "The police carried it off in a bin liner."

"Oh, no!" Gemma's hand went to her mouth and her eyes instantly filled with tears.

"When?" Sunita asked. "*When*?"

"Saturday afternoon when she was shopping and…"

"But Nelson didn't go missing until Sunday," Carli said quickly. "Honestly, Christie, you scared us."

After lunch, the class bustled back into school with Ms Drury flapping behind them in her new open sandals.

Lauren lifted her desk lid to get out her exercise books. Suddenly she let out a shrill cry of surprise. The class swung round to stare at her, and Ms Drury looked up startled.

"Who was that?" she asked. "What's going on?"

Lauren held up a wet black swimsuit.

A Challenge for Lauren

Ms Drury blinked her eyes. "Why have you brought a wet swimsuit to school, Lauren?"

"I didn't," Lauren spluttered.

"Then why are you waving it in the air like that?"

"I found it in my desk. I don't know where it came from. It isn't mine."

Water dripped on to the floor and Lauren held it as far away from herself as she could, to prevent it from drenching her school books and clothes. She stared dismally at her family tree. It was ruined, little more than a damp smudge.

"Take it to the toilets," Ms Drury squealed. "We can't have puddles all over the classroom."

"But I didn't put it there," protested Lauren, her eyes flashing. "It's nothing to do with me."

Some of the other girls began to giggle.

"Tut, tut, Lauren, what are you up to?" said Marga in a loud whisper.

Lauren felt anger rising inside her. It was obvious that Alex had put it there.

"We'll talk about this at the end of the day, Lauren," Ms Drury said firmly.

Lauren swung round to stare at Alex, who shot her a hard stare in return. But Charlotte couldn't contain her pleasure. She grinned at Marga and the two gave a thumbs up sign to each other.

When school ended for the day, Lauren stayed

behind in class to talk to her teacher.

"Don't bother waiting," she told the others. "I'll catch you up at Gemma's. I shouldn't be long, there's nothing really to tell."

She repeated her story to Ms Drury concluding, "It really isn't my swimsuit and I don't know where it came from."

"But do you have any idea who might have put it there?" Ms Drury asked, kindly.

Lauren shook her head. She couldn't blame Alex because she didn't have any proof. Alex would deny everything anyway and be sure to make things worse for her in the future.

Ms Drury looked concerned. "Lauren, if anything is worrying you, you know you can always come and talk to me."

"Thanks," said Lauren. "I will."

Lauren walked across the school playground feeling angry and tired. She was so deep in thought that she didn't see the crowd waiting for her at the school gates.

"Going swimming?" Charlotte asked, stepping out of nowhere.

"Brought in a swimsuit today, did you?" Marga sniggered, also blocking her path.

"A *wet* swimsuit?" Alex corrected her.

"Leave me alone," Lauren rounded on Alex.

"How would you like it if I did the same to you?"

Alex's brother Zack, who had come to meet her from school, pushed his face close to Lauren's.

"You threatening my sister?" he bellowed, his face screwed into a sneer. "You'd better watch out, Miss Captain!" He spat on the ground. "Or anything could happen." Zack shoved Lauren against the gates. Her school bag slipped off her shoulder, and he grabbed hold of the straps.

"Leave me alone!" Lauren shouted. "Let go!" She tugged at the bag until one of the straps snapped. Then Zack let go of the other strap so suddenly that she stumbled backwards and almost fell. Lauren began to run as fast as she could, their laughter ringing out behind her.

Anya had just arrived at Gemma's house to help look for Nelson, when they all saw Lauren thundering down the road towards them.

"That pig! That rotten pig!" she shouted.

"No, we're looking for a dog, remember?" Carli joked.

"I don't care about the dog," Lauren snarled. "I'm talking about Alex Marshall. I'm going to get her. I'm going to *really* get her!"

She told them what had happened at the school

gates.

"You're right," said Anya. "We have to work out a plan."

"But not now," Gemma wailed. "First, can we please go and look for the dog."

"Oh, you and that stupid dog," Lauren snapped. "What about me?"

"I'm worried sick and Mrs Crick's going mental, Lauren. We've *got* to find Nelson today," Gemma pleaded.

"Yeah, try and calm down, Lauren," Sunita joined in. "Looking for Nelson will take your mind off Alex."

"We can work out a plan as we walk," Anya added.

"Anyway, Lauren," said Carli with a little smile. "You're a team captain – you should be heading this search party!"

"I suppose I should," Lauren agreed. "All right then. I'll go and get Bart to come and help us!" she grinned.

Lauren emerged with her dog, Bart, who immediately jumped up licking everyone's hands, knees or cheeks – whichever he could reach. The cheeky mongrel strained on his lead as the group walked towards the park. When Lauren let him off at the park gates, he shot off into the distance, chasing after squirrels and birds.

They checked out every corner of the park and all around the pond. When they came to a play area, Anya flopped on to a swing. "I'm so tired," she said, faintly. "Let's stay here for a while."

"If you all sit on the roundabout, I'll push it," said Lauren. "I need to keep exercising."

"How's that going to help us find Nelson?" said Gemma.

"Change the record, Gems," said Lauren, pushing Anya round faster and faster.

Sunita came up to Gemma and put an arm round her.

"Sunita," asked Gemma, "what if something terrible has happened to him?"

"I bet he's having a great time," Carli suggested, without much enthusiasm. "Wouldn't you if you managed to get away from Mrs Crick?"

"But what if someone stole him or drove off with him in a car? He could be hurt or lost or..."

"But he isn't," said Sunita. "There he is!"

Lauren was over to join them in a flash. "*Where*?"

"Hey, what about me?" wailed Anya, spinning at high speed on the roundabout. "I feel sick!"

The others were too excited to listen. Way across the park, they could see a tiny dog chasing after

birds and squirrels. He ran up to a group of people and made circles round their ankles so that they couldn't move in any direction. Then he dashed off, chasing one dog after another, even those that were twice his size. All the time he was yapping madly.

"It *is* Nelson," Gemma said. "Quick! Let's catch him. *Run!*"

"I can't even walk in a straight line," moaned Anya, before collapsing face down on to the grass.

"Nelson! Nelson!" Gemma called as she ran, but the little dog acted as if he'd never seen her before. He took one look at the four girls heading towards him and tore off in the opposite direction, disappearing into a clump of bushes.

"Go get him, Bart!" Lauren commanded. For once, Bart obeyed her and dashed into the bushes. Seconds later he sprang out again with Nelson close behind him, nipping at his legs. Bart ran back to the girls and trampled over Anya, who squealed, but Nelson shot off back into the bushes.

The girls crashed in after the Chihuahua, scratching their legs. They split up and took different paths through the undergrowth, zigzagging between the trees and bushes. But Nelson was nifty and, although each one of them caught sight of him from time to time, he was never in sight long enough for anyone to grasp hold of his collar.

"He's over here," Anya called, weakly, from beside the roundabout. By the time the girls had raced back to join her, Nelson had disappeared again.

"Just *look* at me!" wailed Anya as she stood up dizzily, her new tracksuit covered in grass stains and muddy paw prints.

Just then, Nelson darted out of the nearby flowerbeds and chased after Bart, who barked as the smaller dog ran energetically in and out of his legs, yapping.

"Come here, Bart!" Lauren shouted. But Bart couldn't get away from Nelson. Lauren managed to grab Bart's collar and yanked him towards her. Gemma made to catch Nelson, but once more he raced away until his little figure was swallowed up by the shrubbery.

"We're *never* going to catch him," Carli said.

"I wish he'd *stayed* lost!" muttered Anya, clutching her arms and panting.

"We'd better get back," said Lauren. "Mum will think something has happened to us."

Reluctantly, Gemma followed her friends. She kept twisting round to look behind her, hoping that Nelson might be following them.

While she was still looking back, she heard Anya shout. *"There he is!"*

She swung round just in time to see Nelson dart into Mrs Crick's front garden. Gemma sprinted into the garden after him and rang the doorbell. Mrs Crick opened the door. Nelson immediately dashed past her into the house, where he ran the length of the hall twice before nosing his way into the sitting room.

"Nelson! Stop! Come here!" Mrs Crick shouted, relief showing in her eyes. Mud and chaos followed the dog through the house, and at first she didn't know whether to be happy or cross.

Above the noise, Gemma tried to explain to her neighbour how they had chased Nelson endlessly round the park.

"The thing is, he loves being out," she ended, as Mrs Crick finally caught hold of him and patted the Chihuahua against her. "In fact, he really needs more exercise..." Gemma blushed as she realised Mrs Crick might take this the wrong way. "If you like, I could take him for a walk," she hurried on, "whenever Lauren goes out with Bart."

For the first time ever, Mrs Crick's face broke into a warm smile. "I've got arthritis so I can't walk far," she said. "Nelson would love a young pair of legs to walk him." Then she frowned all over again. "But you're to take proper care of him young lady, and always keep him on a lead!" And with that, she disappeared back inside and closed the door.

"Huh! Gratitude!" said Carli.

"Nelson might love it, but Bart won't," Lauren complained as the girls headed for home. "Honestly, Gemma, why did you have to say we'd take him for walks? You're nuts."

"OK, OK, I might be nuts, but that poor dog needs exercise. Bart will soon get used to him."

"Oh, will he?" Lauren retorted. "You know my dog better than me, do you? Well I don't want to go for any walks with that stupid Nelson *or* you."

She stomped up the path to her house, went inside and slammed the door behind her.

"Oh not again!" Gemma turned to her friends in dismay. "I can't say anything right."

"Never mind," Sunita advised. "Let her cool down. You know she doesn't mean it."

"Yeah," agreed Carli. "I think that thing with Alex today upset Lauren more than she let on."

"I suppose I wasn't a very supportive best friend," sighed Gemma.

"Only 'cause you were so worried about Nelson," Sunita pointed out.

"Anyway, he's back now," grinned Anya. "So you can all concentrate on supporting me and Lauren at the swimming club!"

Chapter 6

The friends all hit the Sports Centre on Saturday – even Sunita managed to join them, having worn down her gran with her constant pleading. Today, Peter was going to decide on the name for the swimming club.

"I've had lots of suggestions," he said, holding a piece of paper. "I'll read them out and then we can take a vote."

Gemma and Carli eyed each other, nervously.

"The Northborough Swimming Sensations..." began Peter. Only a couple of hands went up and Lauren noticed a lanky boy blush.

"The Northborough Sharks..." continued the coach. A flurry of hands went up this time, and Carli and Gemma exchanged worried glances.

"The Northborough Dolphins..." The friends

each held their breath as more than half the crowd put up their hands.

"It seems we have a clear winner," said Peter. Gemma and Carli whooped and danced in a circle.

Carli plucked up courage, raised her hand and asked, "Is it all right if I have a go at designing a poster, Peter?"

"That would be great! Cheers!" Peter smiled at her.

Sunita, who had brought along her sketchpad and pencils, immediately started making sketches for T-shirts and swimsuits.

"Aha, I see the great designer is at work," Gemma teased, craning over her shoulder.

When the training session was over and the fun hour began, Lauren stayed close to her friends. But Alex Marshall and her crowd still refused to leave her alone. They raced alongside her or swam across her path and there were too many children and floats for the attendants to see what they were up to.

"I voted we should be called the Sharks," Alex told her, menacingly. "They're a lot more... *dangerous* than smelly old dolphins. Know what I mean?" Splashing Lauren in the face with her feet, she swam away.

"Just you wait, Marshall," muttered Lauren to

herself. "Just you wait."

"Got any cheese and chive crisps, Gems?" asked Lauren, sprawled on the Gordons' sofa.

"Oh, yes, Captain, certainly, Captain," obliged Gemma, cringing before her friend and making the others laugh.

"That's OK then," Lauren nodded.

It was Sunday afternoon, and the gang had gathered at Gemma's house. For their project on 'Changes', Sunita, Carli, Lauren and Gemma had brought along photographs of themselves when they were little.

"Look how fat my cheeks were," Sunita wailed, holding up a photograph of herself aged four.

"You looked like a hamster!" giggled Carli.

"She still does!" said Lauren, cheekily. Sunita grabbed a bag of crisps and threw it at her. "No, no, no, these are salt and vinegar!" Lauren complained, chucking them back.

"She may have looked like a hamster, but you were completely bald!" Anya laughed, pointing to a picture of Lauren as a baby.

"And you were really cute when you had bunches and only one front tooth," Sunita told

Carli.

"I wish I was doing your project," Anya sighed. "But our topic this term is conservation. I mean it's local environment and all that, but it's not very interesting."

"But you could bring in animal welfare," Gemma said.

"Do you never think of *anything* but animals?" teased Anya.

"What about car fumes and pollution?" Sunita suggested.

"And saving the rainforests and all that..." said Carli.

Soon they were talking excitedly about ways to improve things. They kept interrupting each other with new ideas, all except Lauren, who seemed to withdraw into herself.

"Lauren, what's the matter?" Gemma asked. "Not keen on being green?"

"Oh, yeah, I suppose so..." said Lauren. "I was just thinking about something else."

"Or some*one* else?" Sunita said, knowingly.

Lauren nodded. "I was thinking it would be great to dump a huge bag of rubbish into Alex Marshall's desk!" she said.

"Imagine her face when she saw it!" Anya squealed.

A Challenge for Lauren

"And then I'd pile a huge bucket of dustbin slops all over her," said Lauren, warming to her theme.

"Come on, Lauren, you know you couldn't do that..." Gemma began.

"Why not?" Lauren snapped. "Why shouldn't I do something to get her back for what she's been doing to me."

Gemma sighed. Why couldn't Lauren ever learn? "Because if you do, you'll get into trouble and she'll just get worse."

"Oh, you're a great help, aren't you? Just like when Anya was getting hassle off her half-brother!" Lauren put on a silly, whining voice: "You mustn't get him back, Anya, you'll only get in trouble!"

"Well, she *did*!" chimed in Carli.

"I almost got him though!" retorted Anya, hotly.

"Everyone just shut up a sec," shouted Sunita, annoyance in her voice. The room fell silent. "We know Alex is a rotten old pig, yeah?"

"You can say that again," Carli said. "I don't know what I would have done without you lot when she was bullying me."

"I've been bullied too," said Sunita. "And I know you're probably right, Gemma, but we've got to stick together here. Agreed?"

"Sorry Lauren," murmured Gemma. "I just don't want to see you come to any more grief, that's all."

Lauren squeezed her friend's arm. "I'm sorry too. It's OK. I can handle her hard-girl act. She doesn't scare me."

"We just have to remember we should always be here for each other," said Anya, with a seriousness that quite surprised her friends. They all nodded and linked little fingers.

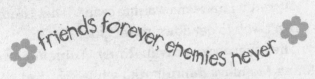
friends forever, enemies never

Monday was another hot day. When the lunch bell rang at school Lauren gave a big thumbs up sign to her friends.

"Before you all vanish," said Ms Drury, stopping her pupils at the classroom door. "I need a volunteer to take down pictures and pin up our new display."

For a few moments there was silence. Then, to everyone's amazement, Charlotte Derring put up her hand.

"I'll do it, Miss," she said. "I don't mind helping."

"Thank you, Charlotte. That's very kind." Ms Drury blinked in surprise.

Charlotte grinned at Alex, and Marga sniggered. Then the class piled out towards the canteen.

During lunch break Lauren chatted to Tania and Katie who were also in the swimming squad. They discussed arm and leg movements, starts and turns and racing dives. Carli showed them all her sketches for the swimming poster.

"The dolphin is wicked," Tania exclaimed.

"It really makes me want to swim," said Lauren. "I can't *wait* to get down to the pool!"

The afternoon passed slowly. Lauren always found Mondays difficult, and while she tried hard to concentrate, her whole body strained to be diving into the cool water.

At last, the bell for home time rang out. Lauren leapt up and grabbed her swimming bag.

"Bye! Have a good swim," her friends called after her, as Lauren rushed for the door, and raced across the playground to the gates.

Her mum was waiting in the car with Harry. "We've got to collect Ben before we can go to the pool," she reminded Lauren. "He needs to be at the Sports Centre too, for the tennis club."

"But can't you drop me off first?" Lauren

begged. "Please, Mum. Please!"

"It'll only take a few minutes," Mrs Standish said calmly. "I'll take you both to the Sports Centre, then Harry and I need to head off to the supermarket. The water won't have drained out of the plughole, you know!"

Finally Mrs Standish dropped them at the Sports Centre. Lauren tumbled out of the car and raced off to the changing rooms.

Alex, Charlotte and Marga were already there, stuffing their belongings into the lockers. Alex stared hard at Lauren, then sniffed and said in an extra loud voice to her sidekicks, "All of a sudden there's a strange smell around. Let's get out of here."

"Yeah," said Marga. "Zack's out there waiting to coach you. If he gets a whiff of this pong, he might be put off." Laughing, they hurried out to the pool in a close huddle.

Lauren felt a rush of anger, but didn't say a word. Gemma was right. Let Alex play her stupid games, *she* was better than that. She quickly opened a cubicle and began to undress. She pulled the towel out of her swimming bag and unrolled it to find her swimsuit.

But the swimsuit wasn't there.

Lauren searched in her bag and all around the

A Challenge for Lauren

floor, but she couldn't see it anywhere. In panic, she even shook the bag upside down, but all that fell out was an empty sweet wrapper. Lauren hurriedly got dressed again and retraced her footsteps to see if she had dropped her costume on the way in.

Eventually, close to tears, she went up to the reception.

"Has anyone handed in a navy blue swimsuit?" she asked.

The receptionist shook her head. "Would you like to borrow one from lost property?"

"All right, I'll have a look," said Lauren, desperately. But as she sorted through the motley array of old swimsuits, she felt herself flushing. She was Lauren Standish, the captain of the girls' team – what would people say if she turned up in some grotty costume the wrong size for her? Alex would never let her live it down...

Tears welled up in her eyes, and she wiped them away furiously. She couldn't face the squad. Not like that. And she couldn't bear the thought of Alex seeing her so upset. She turned and walked away from the Sports Centre without another word.

Lauren waited for a bus, but it didn't come, so she slowly walked all the way home, dragging her swimming bag behind her. Her mother had just arrived and was unloading the shopping with Harry. As Lauren walked into the kitchen, her little brother upended a bag of flour. Fine white powder poured onto the floor and fluttered over Harry's black trousers and their mother's blue skirt.

"Oh, no!" Mrs Standish screamed, grabbing the flour from the toddler. Harry had spent the last hour filling the supermarket trolley with foods she didn't want – this was the last straw. Suddenly she turned pointedly to Lauren. "Hey, what are you doing back so soon? Why aren't you swimming?"

"Because I didn't have my costume," Lauren announced, through gritted teeth. "I thought it might be in the car."

"There's nothing in the car. I just cleared the back seat. Maybe you left it in your bedroom this morning."

"I didn't. I put it in my bag, I know I did." She scowled. "Unless Ben or Harry took it out, of course."

"Don't blame your brothers," her mother scolded. "Go and check upstairs."

Lauren thumped up to her room and rummaged through her drawers and under the bed, even in the dirty laundry basket. The navy blue swimsuit had completely disappeared.

Lauren stomped back down the stairs two-at-a-time and marched out of the house, into Gemma's garden next door.

Gemma and her little sister Lucy were letting the rabbits roam about the garden, and Lucy chased off after them the instant Lauren arrived. Lucy knew that she would find out much more about what her big sister and Lauren were up if she listened from a distance than if she tried to stay nearby. Breathlessly she waited to hear what Lauren had to say.

Lauren's mouth twisted with anger and the words tumbled out in a rush as she explained to Gemma what had happened.

"I just couldn't believe the costume wasn't there," she exclaimed. "I know I wrapped it in the towel this morning and put it in the swimming bag. And I didn't open the bag again until I was at the pool."

"Maybe it fell out somewhere on the way," Gemma said.

"Or someone took it out. Someone who wants to mess things up for me."

"Alex…" said Gemma, grimly. "But when could she have done it?"

"She could have got Charlotte to do it when she stayed behind at lunch. Remember how even Ms Drury was surprised when Charlotte volunteered, and then Alex and Marga sniggered."

"They're always sniggering about something."

"But Charlotte could have easily taken it when Ms Drury went to the staff room," Lauren pointed out.

"I suppose so," Gemma agreed. "But…"

"I'm going to get my own back, Gems. I just *have to*."

"Oh Lauren…" began Gemma.

Lauren's eyes grew large and her nostrils flared. "How many times have we been through this?" she yelled. "I can't let her walk all over me, I've got to do something. And if you don't want to help me, I'll do it on my own."

Before Gemma could say another word, she turned and strode back into her own garden. Lauren stamped up to her bedroom and slammed the door. 'People say they'll help,' she thought. 'But nobody really does. So much for best friends!'

She turned the CD player up to full volume, making the whole house shake to the sound of her music.

When she'd come off the boil a little, Lauren decided Anya would be most likely to be on her side over this one. She called her friend up, and wasn't disappointed.

"How about if we post nasty things through

A Challenge for Lauren

Alex's letter box? Cold chips and stuff?" Anya suggested.

"Brill!"

"You'd have to pick them up first, though, of course. Ugh!" Anya shuddered.

Lauren grinned. "No problem. And we could put chips in her shoes when she's changing."

"And into her swimming cap so that they squash into her hair when she pulls it on."

"They'd probably fry knowing how greasy her hair is!" Lauren chuckled.

"Right!" said Anya. "We'll start collecting chips. But Lauren, if you want to go swimming this week, you can always borrow my bikini."

"Thanks," said Lauren. "But Mum says she'll take me into town Wednesday after school to buy a new costume."

Just as they were about to set off to town on Wednesday, Mrs Standish's car broke down. She immediately phoned Gemma's dad, Garry, who worked for Arches' Autos. He booked the car into the garage for the next day, but the clutch had gone and it would take a few days to fix.

"I'm so sorry, Lauren," Mrs Standish apologised. "The shops will be closed by the time you catch a bus into town. We're completely stuck! Maybe one of your friends has a swimsuit you could borrow?"

"But I don't want someone else's," Lauren stamped her feet. "I'm the captain! I want to have my own!"

At school her friends tried to calm her down.

"You could try wearing mine," Gemma offered.

"Way too small!" moaned Lauren. "No way."

"What about mine?" suggested Sunita. "We're similar heights. I just have to ask Mum to find it," she said. "I think she put it away in a suitcase."

"Great," said Lauren, forlornly. "Thanks."

But by Friday, Lauren was desperate. "Please, please tell me that you've brought it," she said to Sunita. "I have to go swimming. I have to."

"Hang on a minute." Sunita was rummaging through her satchel in the cloakroom area. "Of course I've got it. It's squashed under my lunchbox."

She pulled out her green costume – and as she did so, a pen flicked out and rolled across the floor.

"Oh no!" she cried. "That's my best pen. Where'd it go?"

She dived down on her hands and knees and started crawling across the cold cloakroom floor searching for her pen. Her friends joined in the pen hunt, pushing aside jackets and sweaters that had fallen off the hooks.

"Got it!" called Gemma, holding up the mottled red pen.

"That's great!" said Sunita. "And look what *I've* found." She held up a scrunched, dusty, navy blue swimsuit. "It was under the radiator."

Lauren took the costume, speechless at first.

"It must have dropped out of your bag on Monday and been swept aside by the cleaners," decided Gemma.

Sunita shrugged. "It could've, I guess."

"Nice try, Gemma," said Lauren, batting her dusty costume against the wall. "I think we *all* know who's responsible for *this*."

Chapter 7

"**C**ome on, Anya!"

Lauren banged on the door, impatiently. Saturday morning had come round at last, and her dad's car was chugging at the end of the drive, waiting to take them both off to swimming training.

At last, Anya opened the door, her hair pushed back untidily in a pink banana clip and her pale blue track suit specked with dust. She was surrounded by bulging black dustbin liners and piles of books and clothes.

"Come on, Anya. Let's go," Lauren said. "We'll be late!"

"I didn't realise the time," Anya stepped back and rubbed her forehead. "I've got such a headache. Mum had a big spring clean," she said.

A Challenge for Lauren

Best Friends

"And she shoved everything into these bags for the dustman." Anya's eyes opened wide. "I mean, would you believe it! She was going to throw all these things away without sorting anything out first. And there's me doing a conservation project! These things have to be sorted and recycled don't they?"

"Yeah, yeah," said Lauren. "You're right. But you can't sort them out now. Do it afterwards."

"I'm right in the middle of it now," said Anya. "I can't just leave it like this." She rubbed her forehead again. "You go on without me, and tell Peter I'll definitely be there next week."

"You'd better be," Lauren told her. As captain she didn't feel it was right that Anya should miss a training session, but she didn't want to stop and argue with her friend now. If she didn't get in a pool and swim soon, she would probably explode.

The minute Lauren's body slid into the water, she felt her worries slipping away. Her arms and legs moved smoothly through the pool, and she managed to lower her personal best timings and go faster than ever before.

As she finished her length, Peter called the

84

swimmers to the diving blocks for diving practice.

"A good start makes all the difference to a race," he said. "And from now on I'm going to use the starting gun, so that you get used to the sound it makes."

When it was Lauren's turn to dive, she stepped onto the block, bent forward and waited for the gun. Alex Marshall was standing behind her. Just as the gun went off Alex kicked the starting block. Lauren was so shocked that she lost her balance and landed in the water with a heavy belly flop. Charlotte had stepped across to Peter to ask him to tighten her goggles, so the coach didn't see what happened. He turned back in time to see Lauren splash clumsily into the water.

"You'll be allowed two false starts, Lauren," he said. "Then you'll be disqualified. And in a relay race the whole team would be disqualified. You *have* to get off to a good start."

"But someone kicked the block," Lauren spluttered, her face red with embarrassment. She felt as if her whole body was on fire.

"OK. Have another go," Peter told her. "And everyone keep away from the blocks."

Behind her, she heard Alex chuckle and whisper, "Our little dolphin can't dive. She won't be captain for long."

Lauren gritted her teeth, seething with anger. She wanted to march up to Alex and slap her, but didn't want to do anything that might make Peter think she was out of control. So she narrowed her eyes and thought of Anya and their plan for the cold chips.

She missed Anya being there and stayed close to Tania and Katie, feeling uncomfortable on her own. As usual, Alex and her crowd were hanging around like a bad smell. While Lauren practised her diving, they huddled together, whispering secretively and glancing over at her. Lauren mistimed her dive again, making a big splash in the water. When she surfaced, she saw Alex laughing.

Lauren suddenly felt afraid, cold all over. How could she be captain and inspire respect with someone like Alex Marshall undermining her at every turn?

She swam back to the poolside and hauled herself up, taking deep breaths. She wouldn't let Alex get to her. She *wouldn't*.

All day Sunday, Lauren raged about Alex. When the friends met at Sunita's house to continue their homework projects, she sat in a corner with Anya hatching plans. Gemma reckoned that by this time, Anya was coming over just for the fun of plotting, not for any possible help with her schoolwork. Still, if her mad plans made Lauren feel any better...

"Mouldy potatoes would be good," Anya said. "With sprouty bits."

"And soft, squashy, over-ripe pears!" Lauren's eyes shone with mischief.

Gemma knew her friends' plans would never be acted out. They were just a way of releasing Lauren's frustrations. She wondered if there was anything she could do. She had stood up against Alex before, but that was when the bully had been picking on Carli and she'd caught her red-handed. If she tried to pick a fight now what good would that do?

Even so, by Monday evening, Gemma wanted to show her best friend that she really did care about her. She thought it might cheer Lauren up if they went cycling together in the park, like they used to.

"I suppose we could bring Bart and Nelson and kill two birds with one stone," Lauren agreed. "Why not?"

They phoned Sunita, who said she would join

A Challenge for Lauren

them soon, then collected Nelson and cycled to the park, where the dogs raced across the grass and chased each other between the legs of some boys playing basketball.

"Get out! Go away," the boys shouted. They bounced the ball after the dogs, who barked at them, then bounded after the girls on their bikes, yapping and leaping up.

"I'm boiling," Gemma panted as she peddled hard to keep level with Lauren.

"Me too," said Lauren, unzipping her tracksuit top. "I wish I'd worn shorts, now!"

"Let's have a rest on the swings," Gemma suggested.

"But I can't leave my bike. I haven't brought my D-lock," said Lauren, frowning.

"Nor have I..." Gemma realised. "Oh, they'll be OK. We can prop them against the fence and keep an eye on them."

They leapt on to the swings and pushed their legs forwards and backwards, swinging higher and higher. Lauren felt herself flying higher than ever. It seemed that someone was pushing her. She looked round and realised someone *was*. Alex Marshall. The fat pig must have crept up behind her. She was holding a choc-ice in one hand and using her other hand to push Lauren's swing.

"Get out of it!" Lauren yelled. "I don't need your help, thank you."

"But I thought you *liked* going high, Miss High-and-Mighty Standish," Alex sneered, pushing even harder.

Gemma leapt off her swing and turned to face Alex. "Pack it in, Marshall," she said, fiercely.

A voice called out. "Whose bike is this, then?" Alex's brother, Zack, was standing by the fence with his hands on Lauren's mountain bike.

"It's mine," shouted Lauren. "Leave it alone."

"Oh, I've just remembered," Zack grinned up at her, holding his finger to his chin. "This is *my* bike. I left it here earlier."

"It's *not* your bike," Lauren screamed. "It's *mine*!"

Zack wheeled the bike away from the fence and twirled it around. "Very nice," he said. "Very nice indeed."

"Stop pushing the swing," Lauren shouted to Alex. "I want to get off."

But Alex, who had now finished her choc-ice used both hands to push still harder. "If I owned a bike as nice as that, I'd get a lock. But then some people are just stupid." She glared at Gemma. "Aren't they, Gordon?"

"I told you," Gemma said, her voice wavering.

"Stop pushing her!"

But Alex only shoved harder. "Make me."

"He's pinching my bike, Gems!" Lauren shouted. "Stop him."

Gemma moved towards him, but she was too late. Zack pushed the bike forward and leapt into the saddle. "Bye girls," he waved. "Have a good swing!"

"Come back!" shouted Lauren. In desperation, she let go of the swing's chains and made a jump for it.

"Lauren!" yelled Gemma.

Lauren flew through the air and fell badly on the grass, letting out an agonised scream as her ankle twisted beneath her.

Alex ran off, laughing, while Gemma rushed over to help her friend. "Are you all right? Are you hurt?" she asked.

"Never mind *me*! Get my bike. Stop him!"

Sunita and her brother, Vikram, heard Lauren's screams and shouts as they cycled towards the swings. Spotting Zack riding Lauren's bike, they made straight for him. When he saw the two of them coming at him, Zack threw down the bike and strolled off, laughing. "Oh, silly me. This is a little *girl's* bike!" he guffawed.

Sunita rushed over to Gemma and Lauren.

A Challenge for Lauren

"Can you get up?" she asked. "Can you walk?"

"I don't think so," Lauren shook her head. Her ankle felt hot and painful. If Vikram hadn't been there she would have cried. But she really liked Sunita's brother, and didn't want him to see her as a silly girl who burst into tears at the slightest thing.

"I've twisted my ankle," she mumbled.

"Will you be all right for the gala?" asked Sunita, worriedly.

"I can't let this stop me," said Lauren, wincing with pain. "If I do, it means Alex really has beaten me!"

Chapter 8

Lauren hobbled home, leaning on Vikram's shoulder and grimacing with pain whenever her foot touched the ground. Behind her, Gemma and Sunita pushed the bikes.

"If only we'd arrived sooner," Sunita sighed.

"I wish *I'd* been more use," said Gemma, chewing her lip. "Lauren will go mad if she can't swim."

Mrs Standish rested Lauren in an armchair in the sitting room and put ice cubes in a handkerchief, which she wrapped round her ankle. Later, Lauren held a pack of frozen peas there instead. The ankle swelled up immediately, throbbing with pain.

The following morning when Lauren stared down at her ankle, she wanted to cry – it was bruised and badly swollen. She placed her foot on the ground and winced.

"I'm taking you to the doctor for a check-up," her mother announced.

"Why? You don't think it's broken, do you?" Lauren asked in alarm.

"I don't think anything," said her mum. "I want it looked at. That's all."

The thirty-minute wait at the surgery was almost as painful as the ankle itself. When Lauren finally saw the doctor, he carefully felt all around the swollen joint.

"It isn't broken," he said. "But it's a nasty sprain. You'll have to take it easy for a while."

He sent her to see the nurse, who bandaged her leg and told her that the best cure for a sprain was RICE.

"Rice!" Lauren exclaimed. "Rice is disgusting!"

"You don't eat it," the nurse explained. "Rice is a way of remembering what you have to do. The R stands for rest, I for ice, C is for compression – that means wearing a bandage – and E is for elevation – which means you should sit down and keep your leg up high."

"But when will I be able to go swimming?"

Lauren asked.

"You really should rest up until your ankle is better," the nurse replied. "The less you do, the quicker it will heal."

Lauren went home and sat in front of the television with her leg propped on a stool. Normally, she'd be thrilled to miss a day's school, but right now she felt miserable. When Gemma called round to ask how she was, she hugged her friend close.

"I feel awful, Gems. I could be stuck like this for ages. I've been told I can't do sport, so now Alex will get her own way. She's bound to be made captain if I'm not there!"

"Then let her be captain," Gemma said suddenly. "Is it really worth putting yourself through all this for one swimming gala?"

"You must be joking!" Lauren flicked her pony tail angrily. "It's about more than just the swimming gala now... and there's no way I'm going to give in to that stupid ratbag!"

The following week Lauren went back to school wearing a bandage with one of her brother's trainers over her bad foot. Her mother drove her

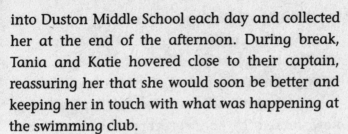

into Duston Middle School each day and collected her at the end of the afternoon. During break, Tania and Katie hovered close to their captain, reassuring her that she would soon be better and keeping her in touch with what was happening at the swimming club.

In another part of the playground, Alex showed off her new haircut. Her thick black hair had been cropped close to her head so that it could fit more easily into the tight swimming caps the squad wore.

"Now I can swim even faster," she said, fixing Lauren with fierce black eyes.

"Ignore her, Lauren," said Sunita, as Alex swaggered away. "Just concentrate on getting better."

"Yeah, you're still the captain, after all," said Gemma. "And, hey, did you see Carli's poster design for the gala?"

"Yeah," said Lauren, trying to calm down. "It's a brill picture, no wonder Peter went for it."

As they headed back to the classroom, Carli asked Sunita about the special T-shirts she'd been working on.

"Gran nearly exploded as usual, but I'm really excited!" Sunita whispered. "Don't tell Lauren about the captain's T-shirt – I'm keeping it a surprise!"

A Challenge for Lauren

"Great," said Carli, grinning.

"Mum," Anya moaned. "Don't do this to me!"

Anya couldn't believe it. The bulging black bags now lurked in the corner of her room like enormous monsters trying to fill every inch of space. Her cuddly toys and pink fluffy footstool were buried beneath them, and now her mum had given her an ultimatum.

"I mean it, Anya," Mrs Michaels said. "I've got to go away on a course for a few days. If the bags are still here when I get back, I'm throwing them all out!"

Anya groaned. She had to sort out the bags, but she knew she couldn't do it alone. She needed some help from her friends. First she rang Sunita and invited her to come round to her house on Sunday and asked her to pass the word on to Carli. Then she pressed the memory button, to bring up Gemma's number.

"I'll come," Gemma replied, "but I don't know about Lauren. Her foot's pretty bad. She's really down."

But Anya was determined to snap her friend out of her mood and to get her round. "*Please* I need your help," she told Lauren down the phone.

"Anya," said Lauren. "You could cover for me. I could say I'm going to yours to help sort stuff out, then you can get your dad to drive me to the pool so I can practise."

"That's such a bad idea, Lauren," said Anya. "You'll do more harm than good if you try to do too much too soon. Anyway, I really *do* need your help!"

"What can I do with only one foot?" Lauren replied, moodily.

"You don't need feet for this," Anya promised. "Just come here. Your mum can bring you over. My mum's away, so Dad's in charge, but she's left an enormous feast."

"OK – better than rotting here anyway," said Lauren. Her spirits couldn't help but lift at the thought of the delicious food Mrs Michaels always provided.

As soon as the friends arrived and Lauren had hobbled across to the sofa, Anya quickly breezed in with a tray of snacks and drinks.

"I'll be back in a few minutes," said Anya, mysteriously.

The girls all waited. Odd rustling sounds were coming from outside the door, then Anya burst in with a black bin-bag in each hand. "Plenty more where these came from!" she said, grinning.

"Why didn't we just go up to your room?" asked Gemma.

Anya stared at her. "You think I could *bear* such a mess in my room?"

"Wonderful," said Sunita. "We love coming to visit you, Anya. It's so glam!"

The others all laughed, but Anya continued regardless. "I want you all to choose anything you want from these bags," she said. "And while you're looking through them, maybe you could sort the things into piles?"

"You're getting us to do *all* your sorting out for you!" Sunita laughed.

"True," Anya agreed. "But doing it together will be fun."

Soon the room was cluttered with piles of clothes, as well as books, ornaments, bottles, shells and all sorts of odd items that the Michaels family had picked up on their travels. Anya handed out gifts to her friends.

"People are always giving me drawing things," she told Sunita and Carli, handing them pads and pens. "I just can't use them all. And Gemma – here's the rabbit sweater I promised you."

"Brill!" Gemma pulled on the sweater and did a

twirl. The others wolf-whistled and laughed.

Eventually, all the bags had been sorted. Anya, Gemma, Sunita and Carli heaved plastic bags full of old newspapers and magazines to the paper bank at the end of the road while Lauren stayed at the house, resting her ankle.

"What are we going to do with the rest of the things?" asked Sunita when they got back. Groups of objects were still strewn in messy mounds all over the living room and across the hall.

"We could hold a kind of jumble sale here to get rid of them," Lauren suggested.

"Yes, yes, let's do that," Anya cried, excitedly.

"We could give the money to the World Wildlife Fund," said Gemma. "Old Mr Jones keeps a tin for it in his corner shop."

"Good idea," said Anya, dusting down her shift dress. "That'll really impress my teachers. And I'll take a photo of you all behind the stall and put it in my project folder too."

They dragged a table to the pavement in front of the house and set out as many of the remaining items as it could hold. Luckily, it was a sunny afternoon with a clear blue sky. The street led down to a pretty riverside walk, and today it seemed that everyone in town was going to the river. Almost everyone stopped to browse at the

girls' table. Anya was busy snapping photos, when a familiar voice boomed out.

"Got any bandages, then?"

Lauren looked up, sharply.

"Ooops, no," a second voice joined in. "All the bandages in town are wrapped round someone's ankle."

And a third voice added, "Going to the swings? Oh dear, I forgot, you don't sit on swings. You jump off them."

Alex, Charlotte, Marga and Zack pushed to the front of the table.

"Only idiots jump off swings," Zack said, roughly elbowing people away. "Let's have a look at your ankle then."

He laughed as Lauren scowled at him. "You weren't a good swimmer before. Now, you're useless. I'm coaching 'em every night and Alex is super fast."

"A snail would seem super fast to your brain cells," said Anya, haughtily.

"Anyway, if Alex is so brilliant," challenged Sunita, "how come Lauren's captain?"

"Lauren won't be captain for much longer," said Charlotte as she jostled to the front of the crowd. "Even if she gets better, she won't be good enough for the gala, will she?"

100

"Yes, she will actually," Anya said defensively. "Peter's got faith in her. He keeps asking how she is."

"Yeah, well, you don't know nothing, do you?" Marga said smugly. "'Cause *Alex* is gonna be captain now."

They all began to walk away, Zack slyly pocketing a glass paperweight.

"No she's not. *I'm* captain," Lauren shouted, her face blotchy with anger. "I'll be back and swimming any day now and I'll be better than the lot of you. You can't scare me off! You hear me, Marshall?"

She pushed the table away and limped after Alex and her friends. They laughed and began to run, hoping that she would try and chase after them. But Sunita and Carli held her back.

"Don't," Sunita said. "That's what they want you to do. You'll do your ankle in even more and it'll take *ages* to heal."

"I *hate* them," Lauren said, tears in her eyes. "How can Alex be captain?"

"They were just winding you up," said Carli. "Don't believe a word."

"Yeah?" said Lauren, bitterly. "Well, how long before it becomes the truth?"

Chapter 9

Every day Lauren got out of bed praying that her leg would be better. But she still flinched everytime her foot touched the ground.

One morning, wondering for the millionth time if her ankle would *ever* heal, she stood up and for a moment there was no pain. Could it be true?

Tentatively Lauren walked about. She sat down on the bed then stood up again. *Still* no pain. Could it really be true?

"Mum! Mum!" she screamed.

The whole family came running. Ben stormed into the room, Harry crashed through the door, Bart started barking, and Mrs Standish hurried upstairs with her husband close behind her.

"I can walk!" Lauren sang out. "Look, my ankle's totally fine! And if I can walk on it, I can definitely swim!"

Her friends were delighted when they saw Lauren, but they didn't like the idea of her going to the Sports Centre on her own.

"You should ask your brother Ben to go with you," Anya suggested. "Alex's brother coaches her, so why shouldn't Ben coach you?"

Ben, however, wasn't so keen on the idea. "I can't. I've got tennis lessons after school, and when I don't have tennis, I've got homework."

"Thanks a million!" Lauren exploded. "Alex's rotten brother Zack helps her but my so-called *nice* brother can't be bothered to help me!"

Lauren fumed all evening, until Sunita phoned.

"Lauren, look you don't need to ask Ben," she said.

"I already have," Lauren interrupted. "And the brat said no. Brothers are a pain in the neck!"

"They're not," Sunita stopped her. "My brother Vikram has volunteered to coach you whenever you want!"

"Vikram! Really? *Vikram* said that?" Lauren couldn't believe her luck. Vikram was a fantastic at sports, and played in the school team at football, rugby, tennis and cricket. If he wasn't so busy, he'd

A Challenge for Lauren

be in the squad for the swimming gala too.

She rushed downstairs to tell Ben, but he stopped her before she could open her mouth.

"I've been thinking," he said. "I *will* help you, Lauren. I'll come swimming whenever I can. Anything to keep that loser Zack off your back."

Lauren flung her arms around her brother in delight. "With two brothers helping me, Alex Marshall and her rotten brother Zack can go take a running jump!"

Over the next few days, Lauren felt better and better. Each day after school Vikram or Ben went with her to the pool, staying to coach her whenever they could. Zack was usually there too, yelling at his sister and bullying her constantly to 'swim faster' and 'pull stronger'.

At first, Lauren used a float to practise leg-kicks and gradually build up the strength in her legs. Or she used a pull-buoy, which supported her legs really well and allowed her to concentrate on her arm movements. Within a fortnight she was swimming easily as well as before her accident.

Alex watched her progress through narrowed eyes, making sure her crew stepped up their name-calling at school.

"Vikram's no match for Zack," Charlotte laughed. "He hardly even knows how to swim."

104

"He's a wimp," Marga said. "Just like his sister," she added, making sure that Sunita heard her.

The day of the swimming gala was drawing near and everything seemed to be running smoothly at last. Then Anya dropped her bombshell.

"Guess what?" she said, brightly. "I'll be starting tap classes next Saturday morning! Astrid went to the first lesson yesterday, and she says it's really cool. I have to join quickly or there may not be any places."

"But you can't go on Saturday," said Lauren, looking up in alarm. "That's when we have swimming club!"

"I'll have to drop swimming then," said Anya, tossing her plaits from her shoulders. "If I don't start now, I might not get a place, and I won't be as good as everyone else."

"But you can't just drop out of swimming like that!" protested Lauren. "You're in the squad!"

"I can do what I like!" retorted Anya.

But Sunita stepped in. "How could you, Anya? You should be ashamed of yourself."

"But I always said I would leave the club when tap classes began," Anya said defensively.

"Well you can't," Gemma added. "We all agreed to help Lauren. You can't let her down now."

"You want our club to win the gala, don't you?" said Carli, scratching her lip nervously. "The squad needs you, Anya."

"OK. OK," Anya took a deep breath. "Everyone stay calm. I'll stay. I'll just have to catch up with the tap later."

"Too right you will!" said Lauren. "Or I'll be putting cold chips in *your* shoes!"

The weekend before the gala, Mrs Standish invited the girls for tea and came up with a brilliant suggestion to take their minds off the event.

"How about a sleepover next Saturday after the gala's over?" she said. "We'll put up tents in the garden and you can have a midnight feast."

"Yes!" the girls chorused at once.

"I'll get some of the latest videos from my dad's shop," Sunita said.

"My mum could make us some sandwiches," offered Carli.

"I'll bring something yummy for pudding," said Anya. "Like chocolate gateaux or toffee ice cream."

"It'll be a great celebration," said Gemma, squeezing Lauren's arm.

"And look," said Sunita, her hands behind her back. "I've got something for you... *Captain Standish!*"

Lauren gasped as Sunita handed her a deep blue T-shirt with the words 'GIRLS' CAPTAIN – NORTHBOROUGH DOLPHINS' emblazoned in yellow across the front.

"It's wicked," she whispered, completely stunned. "What can I say?"

"Oh, 'thank you' will probably do!" laughed Sunita as Lauren hugged her.

As the other girls kicked around wilder and crazier ideas about the sleepover, Lauren held her T-shirt close, a tremor of fear shivering through her. *Would* they be celebrating next Saturday? Or would Alex still find a way to ruin everything for her?

Chapter 10

Lauren woke up before anyone else and threw open her bedroom curtains. It was the day of the gala. She yawned and stretched, shaking her long blonde hair from her eyes. She blinked at the sunlight, hoping it would dazzle away last night's bad dreams.

All night she had dreamt she was swimming. Or rather she'd been kicking her legs and moving her arms through the water, unable to move. Lauren could see the end of the pool ahead of her, but in the nightmare she just couldn't reach it. She woke up with Alex's laughter still ringing in her ears.

Now it was morning. Soon she really would be swimming. And this time she had to reach the end of the pool.

A few hours later Lauren arrived at the Sports

Centre, wearing her new captain's T-shirt. Coaches and cars filled the car park as swimmers and spectators drove up from all over the district.

Gemma, Sunita, Carli and their families were among the first to take their places on the spectator benches. The steamy atmosphere at the poolside added to the tension as they waited for the gala to begin.

"Now I understand why you've been so excited," Carli's mum smiled at her daughter. "Your posters are everywhere!" On every wall, and even hanging from the ceiling of the pool hall, were the posters and banners that Carli had designed.

"Sunita designed the T-shirts the team's wearing," Gemma told them all. "Aren't they cool?"

Sunita blushed and her parents turned to look at her. "Our Sunny is a girl of many talents," Mr Banerjee said, smiling and squeezing his daughter's shoulder.

There was a commotion near the door as a TV crew arrived and began to set up their equipment.

"So it really *is* going to be on the local news," Mrs Standish remarked. "Northborough's not seen an event like this for years."

"When's it going to start then?" Lucy asked,

sulkily. "We've been here ages."

The swimmers were dying for the races to begin, but there was a last minute hitch. The doors to the changing rooms had jammed. A pool handyman was still sorting out the problem when it was time for the competitors to get changed. Peter gathered the squads together and decided to lead them round the pool to the poolside entrance to the changing rooms instead. The crowd cheered as the swimmers marched past, still fully clothed and carrying their backpacks. The Northborough squad all looked particularly smart in their new blue T-shirts.

As they made their way towards the changing rooms, Alex and her cronies moved closer to Lauren. "Push her," Alex whispered to Charlotte. "Trip her up!"

Charlotte stuck out her foot, but, at the same moment, someone at the back pushed forward. In the confusion, it was Alex who tripped and fell. A scream filled the hall, followed by a loud splash. Alex was in the water, fully clothed, her rucksack still over her shoulder. Someone laughed, and another person joined in. They thought it was a joke. But it was no joke for Alex. She was tangled up in the straps of her bag. She wriggled and twisted, but her arms were trapped and she couldn't slide out. She could feel herself being dragged down by the weight of her kit.

Everything seemed to happen at once. A poolside attendant reached for a rescue pole. Peter, who'd been trying to push his way back through the swimmers towards the pool, started to shout for people to clear the way. But then there was another splash. Someone else had dived fully-clothed into the water and was hauling Alex to safety. It was Sunita's brother, Vikram. He loosened the straps on Alex's bag and raised her onto the poolside, where Peter checked she was all right and helped her get her breath back. Shaken and humiliated, Alex stamped off to the changing rooms, the water dripping from her.

Her face grim, Lauren followed her rival. She found Alex slumped on a bench in an empty room.

"Are you all right?" she asked, handing Alex a towel. "Are you hurt?"

Alex spluttered and spat out some water, but shook her head. "I'm fine," she said. "I just nearly drowned, that's all."

Alex was shaken up. She couldn't believe it had

A Challenge for Lauren

Best Friends

been Vikram who had dived in to save her – neither of the brothers she idolised had been quick enough off the mark. And she was amazed that Lauren seemed actually to care whether or not she was OK.

The incident had made Lauren think twice. She realised for the first time exactly what lengths Alex was prepared to go to in order to be captain.

Behind Lauren, Marga and Charlotte had walked in and stood menacingly in the doorway. Then the rest of the squad began to gather around too, waiting for a showdown. But Lauren found herself agreeing with what Gemma had said weeks ago. If Alex really wanted to be captain so much, then, fine – she *could* be. First, though, Lauren had something to say.

"Just what did you think you were doing, Alex?" she began. "You tried to put me out of the race just now and you could really have hurt *both* of us. These last few weeks have been awful... You made me fall off the swings and almost break my ankle. You ruined my homework project with that wet costume. You got your brother to threaten me after school and you stole my swimsuit and hid it, didn't you?"

Alex wiped her hair with the towel and kept her back to Lauren. But she didn't defend herself.

112

"You're *so* out of order," Lauren continued, staring at her. "So desperate to have your own way. Well, being a captain is about leadership. Setting an example. What example do you think *you've* set, Alex?"

Alex said nothing, facing the wall.

"I don't pretend to know it all," Lauren went on. "I just do the best I can. But I want our club to *win* this gala, and if the only way I can trust you to stop mucking up our chances is to make you captain, then, here." She pulled off the captain's T-shirt and thrust it at Alex. "You can *be* captain."

"Yes, yes, yes!" Charlotte and Marga punched the air. "Go for it, Alex. Go for it."

But Alex didn't jump up in triumph or take the T-shirt. She squinted her eyes at the rest of the squad and saw their shocked faces. It was all out in the open now. Lauren had finally offered her what she'd wanted all along, but she knew she couldn't accept it.

"You're captain," she pointed her finger at Lauren. "You'd just better make sure we *do* win."

The teams marched out to the poolside and gathered at their allotted places. The referee called for the first swimmers to take their positions on the diving blocks. A hushed silence filled the hall. He raised the starting gun and fired the first shot. The swimmers flew through the air and hit the water. The crowd leapt to their feet and strained forward to watch. Clapping and cheering echoed around the walls. The gala had begun.

Race followed race. Swimmers competed in the heats for individual strokes and in relay races. Dressed in white, the time-keepers waited at the end of each lane to note the speed of each swimmer. Stroke judges walked slowly down the poolside checking that everyone swam correctly. Turn judges and finishing judges watched for mistakes at crucial moments.

The loudspeaker crackled as the announcer read out each swimmer's timing and parents and coaches made notes in their programmes.

Anya's individual race was the fifty-metres backstroke. She jumped into the pool and grasped the rail, waiting to begin. When the referee said, "Take your marks," she pulled her body forward to the edge of the pool. When the gun sounded she threw her head back, stretched fully, and glided backwards. Then she swam, pulling with her arms and making strong kicking movements with her legs. She approached the wall and went into a spin turn, whipping her legs out quickly and pushing them against the wall, as she went into the second length. She glanced to one side and saw another swimmer practically level with her. When she saw the marker flags above, she knew she was five metres from the end. She put all her strength into one last effort but the other swimmer still reached the wall just ahead of her.

The crowd cheered as the girls climbed out of the pool, feeling dazed. Lauren hurried across to hug Anya. She'd gained second place.

"Up the Dolphins!" Sunita and Carli screamed.

"And she broke her p.b," Gemma said, turning to Mr and Mrs Michaels excitedly as the timings were read out.

"What's a p.b?" Annie asked.

"It means 'personal best'. You know, your fastest timing so far," Carli explained, proudly. She'd only recently learned the term herself.

Between races Lauren wore her captain's T-shirt and joked and chatted with her squad. She wrapped towels round people who shivered as they waited and told them to jog on the spot to warm up before competing. And she was first across to

A Challenge for Lauren

comfort one of the younger swimmers who was disqualified from her race. She did a good dive, but then started to swim with a front crawl kick instead of doing breaststroke.

"I got so muddled up," she sobbed. "I've really messed up now."

"It's all right," Lauren reassured her. "We all make mistakes."

Soon it was time for Alex's race – the fifty-metres butterfly. She got off to a good start and swam well, her strong shoulders working together in the powerful arm action, her feet holding together in a dolphin kick. She did a perfect turn – both hands touching the wall at the same time – and quickly swam the second length, reaching the end and touching the wall seconds before anyone else. Lauren ran up to congratulate her and she smiled at Lauren for what was probably the first time in her life.

When the final for the freestyle race was called, Lauren took her place on the starting blocks and did a perfect racing dive. She glided long beneath the water, going straight into the stroke, her body flat, her head and legs in line. Her hands speared the water without splashing and her legs kicked up and down, toes pointed and ankles loose. She quickly gained rhythm and took on speed as she sliced through the water.

She did a tumble turn, pushing hard with her legs, before setting off on the second length.

She heard the cries of her team-mates and friends. *"Go on, Lauren! Go for it!"*

She used all her last reserves of energy, determination, skill and strength as she reached the final leg of the race. Her fingers touched the wall and she pulled herself out to the sound of mad cheering. She'd done it! She'd won!

Anya ran across to hug her, and Carli, Sunita and Gemma shouted until their throats were sore.

"Dolphins are the best!"

Between the races, the squad kept together. But, as time passed, they began to get restless and tired.

"I'm hungry," Tania moaned.

"So am I," said Anya. "I could eat six iced buns."

"Well, you can't," Lauren told them. "We've still got to swim in the relay."

But when the relay was called, Tania was nowhere in sight. Lauren hurried across to the benches.

"We have to find Tania *now*," she told her friends.

Sunita, Carli and Gemma moved like lightning, searching the crowd, Lucy and Annie hopping along behind them. There were hundreds of people, standing in groups, chatting, looking at the programmes. The noise was deafening, echoing around the vast hall.

It seemed Tania had vanished without trace. Then Annie ran up and tugged at Lauren's T-shirt. "She's in the canteen! I saw her buying a chocolate bar!" she said.

Lauren caught hold of Tania, just as she was about to take a bite.

"Forget it, Tania!" she shouted, throwing the chocolate bar across the room. "Come on, quick! The race is about to start!"

Sheepishly, Tania ran after her captain back to the pool, just in time for the team medley finals.

Anya, Tania, Alex and Lauren took their places, two at each end, each ready to swim a different stroke. Backstroke was first, and Anya jumped into the water, grasped the rail and got off to a good start. Tania took over and kept up the pace, swimming breaststroke. Then Alex pushed them into joint lead with the third stroke – butterfly, while Lauren waited anxiously to swim the final stroke – freestyle.

She waited to dive in, biting her lip. Anxiously,

her eyes fixed on Alex heading towards her, her shoulders heaving up and down, in and out of the water. Everything hinged on this last race. Could she trust her? Or would Alex humiliate her even now, ruining the Dolphins' chances of success?

Around her the spectators were screaming in support of the teams and loud and clear above all others she could hear her friends chanting "*Dolphins! Dolphins!*"

Alex drew near and Lauren narrowed her eyes to watch Alex's hands. She thought she might be sick from the tension. But as Alex's fingers touched the wall, Lauren felt her feet lift off from the diving block almost of their own accord. She plunged into the water and swam with all her might towards the finish, not even daring to glance sideways at the other swimmers. The wall was ahead of her. Her body ached from the exertion. Lauren blinked and kept going, until she gave one last almighty stretch and touched the finishing wall. The roaring of the water in her ears was replaced by the cheering of the crowd. As she hoisted herself out of the pool, the team crowded around her.

A hand clamped down on her shoulder. It was Alex. "We did it! Lauren, we actually *won*!"

The team was a *real* team. The swimmers had done their best, and had made their squad the best

A Challenge for Lauren

– Lauren and her team-mates were the overall winners in their age group. When Lauren stepped up to take the cup for the club and the cameras flashed, it was the happiest moment of her life.

"Well done everyone, that was top work!" Peter shouted as they celebrated afterwards. "A couple of months ago the Northborough Dolphins didn't exist – now we're county champions!"

"Three cheers for Peter," cried Lauren, springing up beside him. "The best coach in the world!"

Everyone cheered, including Peter's tall blonde girlfriend, Maggie, who'd travelled miles to see the gala and now wouldn't leave his side.

Later that night, wriggling into sleeping bags in Lauren's garden, the gang agreed that this had been the best day of the year. Mr Standish had put up two tents on the lawn, one for the girls and one for the boys. Even Sunita, whose brothers were sharing a tent with Lauren's brother, Ben, had been allowed to stay overnight. And Vikram had given Lauren the second-best moment of her life when he came across and congratulated her, kissing her cheek.

It had been a totally fab evening. They had

watched the latest videos and eaten as much delicious food as they could possibly eat, including Anya's desserts and samosas from Sunita's gran.

The sky was clear, lit by thousands of stars.

"I wonder what our next adventure will be," Carli said. "I mean what could *ever* be as exciting as this?"

"Tap dancing?" Anya said. "Astrid says..."

But Lauren picked up a cushion and threw it at her.

"Something's sure to come up," Sunita mused. "It usually does. The main thing is that whatever happens, we're all in it together."

Gemma looked across at Lauren and smiled. "Too right."

The girls formed a circle and were about to link little fingers, when they were interrupted by a strange scraping sound.

"What's that?" whispered Anya.

"A ghost!" teased Sunita.

"It's coming from the fence," said Lauren, puzzled. A little brown dog trotted into view. "Oh, no!"

"Look,"giggled Carli. "It's Nelson, he wants to join in."

"Oh no, not that rat again!" Anya shrieked.

Lauren raised her eyebrows. "Wonderful. Hey,

why don't we get the rabbits out, too?"

"Now, *that's* not a bad idea," Gemma replied.

"If you *mean* that..." said Anya, looking shocked.

But Carli and Sunita couldn't keep straight faces. Soon, they were all giggling. Still laughing, they linked little fingers and chanted with feeling.

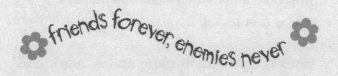

friends forever, enemies never

Friends
FOREVER

When Carli Pike joins Duston Middle School,
she's in for a hard time. Alex Marshall, the
notorious bully, is up to her old tricks again –
she and her sidekicks are determined to turn
the new girl's life into a nightmare.

It doesn't take the Best Friends long to see
that Carli's in trouble, but Lauren loses interest
and Anya is too wrapped up in her flash friend
Astrid. Can Gemma and Sunita find the proof
they need to help Carli survive Duston?

OH
BROTHER!

The half-term break has finally arrived. Anya
plans to shop till she drops! Gemma's chuffed
because she's been allowed to get another pet
rabbit. Lauren just can't wait to play loads
of football.

But the others are seriously depressed.
Sunita's gran is threatening to organise a
private tutor and no one can get a word out of
Carli. The holiday gets even worse when Anya's
half-brother Christopher arrives. Will the Best
Friends manage to hold together?

Spotlight on
SUNITA

When Sunita's attention is caught by a fashion competition on TV, she knows she has to enter. Problem is, she's also got to keep the whole thing top secret. Anya's out to win too, and has wangled the perfect headstart.

During the agonising wait for results, the other Best Friends have worries of their own. Lauren goes through torment when she tries out for the district football team, despite Carli's encouragement. And Gemma? Well, her little sister is driving her *mad*...

More brilliant Best Friends books available from BBC Worldwide Ltd

The prices shown below were correct at the time of going to press. However BBC Worldwide Ltd reserve the right to show new retail prices on covers which may differ from those previously advertised in the text or elsewhere.

1 **Friends Forever** Gill Smith
0 563 38092 6 £2.99

2 **Oh Brother!** Narinder Dhami
0 563 38093 4 £2.99

3 **Spotlight on Sunita** Narinder Dhami
0 563 40552 X £2.99

4 **A Challenge for Lauren** Heather Maisner
0 563 40553 8 £2.99

All BBC titles are available by post from:
Book Service By Post,
PO Box 29, Douglas, Isle of Man, IM99 1BQ

Credit cards accepted.
Please telephone 01624 675137 or fax 01624 670923.
Internet http://www.bookpost.co.uk
or e-mail: bookshop@enterprise.net for details.

Free postage and packaging in the UK. Overseas customers: allow £1 per book (paperback) and £3 per book (hardback).